P9-DMZ-719

THE
SHACK

REFLECTIONS
for every day of the year

"Let me touch your eyes . . ."

THE
SHACK
REFLECTIONS
for every day of the year

windblown
MEDIA

WM. PAUL YOUNG

Copyright © Wm. Paul Young 2012

All rights reserved. Except as permitted under the U.S. Copyright
Act of 1976, no part of this publication may be reproduced,
distributed, or transmitted in any form or by any means, or stored in
a database or retrieval system, without the prior written permission
of the publisher.

Cover and interior design by Koechel Peterson and Associates, Inc.,
Minneapolis, Minnesota

Published in association with Hachette Book Group
237 Park Avenue
New York, NY 10017

Quotes taken from *The Shack* published by Windblown Media
4680 Calle Norte
Newbury Park, CA 91320

Printed in the United States of America

First Edition: October 2012

10 9 8 7 6 5 4 3 2 1

Library of Congress Control Number: 2012939832

To my mother and father,

Henry and Bernice Young,

it will forever be said

of you that you were

a man and woman of prayer.

A Note to the Reader

When I was approached to consider writing this book of responses, Reflections if you will, on quotes taken from *The Shack*, I hesitated. I have always resisted the idea of any sort of study guide for *The Shack*, mostly because it is a work of fiction, a story, a novel that hopefully creates space for folks to hear whatever the Spirit would like to whisper into their hearts at whatever point they have paused in their own journey. A guide tends to show you the places they think are most popular or have been beneficial to them, and you sometimes feel that what once was a river has become a man-made canal taking you to a single destination.

This is not a study guide. There is no set of questions looking for a right answer, no hidden agenda, and no desire to steer the boat to a predetermined port. The value of these quotes and reflections is really up to you, the reader. I don't know you. I don't know what is going on in your life—your joys and challenges. You may be in the center of a devastation or the eye of a hurricane. You might be enjoying the backwaters of an eddy before plunging back into the

rapids. You could be lonely this moment, or despairing, or filled with exhilaration and the rush of success. I simply don't know. But I do know that these quotes have been pulled from a story of authentic humanity, and there is much we share, both in our questions and our process. So this book is an invitation to stop for a moment, to reflect, to consider, to respond, to pray, to remain silent, to cry, to laugh, to share.

If you care to, at the end of the book I have a list of some of my friends who participated with me in "reflecting" on the quotes. We are all ordinary people from different ages, backgrounds, and involvements, but we share with you our uniqueness and our humanity.

Thank you, in advance, for allowing me and some friends to intrude upon your world and for participating with us in a community who desires more . . . more light, more love, more truth, more grace, more kindness, more freedom. Together we will always be more than the sum of our parts.

WM. PAUL YOUNG, AUTHOR OF *The Shack*

1 JANUARY

Mackenzie, it's been a while. I've missed you. I'll be at the shack next weekend if you want to get together.—Papa

Please give me ears to hear your invitation and courage to go with you into places that I would rather not. Oh yeah, Happy New Year!

2

Who wouldn't be skeptical when a man claims to have spent an entire weekend with God, in a shack no less?

Y
ou are such a mystery to me, and to say that your ways are above our ways and your thoughts above ours doesn't even qualify as an understatement. As best I know how, I open me to what you want to do in my life, even when I can't begin to understand it. I believe, but please help my unbelief.

Suffice it to say that while some things may not be scientifically provable, they can still be true nonetheless.

You keep talking about love and trust and relationship, and I want proof. I confess what actually matters most to me I will never find in a test tube or petri dish, but I also confess that I want the control that proof seems to offer. Help!

I will tell you honestly that being a part of this story has affected me deep inside, in places I had never been before and didn't even know existed; I confess to you that I desperately want everything Mack has told me to be true.

Wow, I am still such an unbeliever. I know you see my faith for what it truly is, and you know I want my trust to grow. I do believe . . . more now than ever, but please would you gently hold me, even while I doubt and express a lack of trust?

5 JANUARY

Mack would like you to know that if you happen upon this story and hate it, he says, "Sorry . . . but it wasn't primarily written for you." Then again, maybe it was.

It scares me to think of asking you to do whatever it takes to build authenticity in me. I am quite sure I am going to hate it. And yet, here I go, asking . . . and now why am I crying? This seems so stupid, but please, look past my reactions and give me what is good.

He wanted a narrative to help him express to them not only the depth of his love, but also to help them understand what had been going on in his inside world. You know that place: where there is just you alone—and maybe God, if you believe in him. Of course, God might be there even if you don't believe in him. That would be just like him.

To think that you are in my "inside world," my secret place. Please let me know that you like being there with me, even more than I like being there.

7

I suppose that since most of our hurts come through relationships so will our healing, and I know that grace rarely makes sense for those looking in from the outside.

I don't understand how you bring healing into my life or how grace works. You know where I come from, and why trust is so difficult for me. Please help me grow in believing that you are good, all the time, and will always do what is best.

The thing is, he usually makes uncomfortable sense in a world where most folks would rather just hear what they are used to hearing, which is often not much of anything. . . . When he does talk, it isn't that they stop liking him—rather, they are not quite so satisfied with themselves.

So many of us are scared to death and clinging to anything that gives an imagination of comfort. Who wants to be uncomfortable, especially when those around you begin saying you are mad for asking questions and disturbing the systems? Please be courageous in me.

9 JANUARY

Papa . . . There it was. Papa was Nan's favorite name for God and it expressed her delight in the intimate friendship she had with him.

I have a ways to go, but I do want to become comfortable in your affection, so please whisper your name to my soul, that name just for you and me.

Mack's heart was suddenly penetrated by unexpected joy. A sunset of brilliant colors and patterns played off the few clouds that had waited in the wings to become central actors in this unique presentation. He was a rich man, he thought to himself, in all the ways that mattered.

Thank you for those moments that seem to bypass our minds and reach into the deep and precious places that push us to contemplate the true and real, that sing to us that life is good! Open my heart and heal me.

Mack could lie and gaze up into that vastness for hours. He felt so incredibly small yet comfortable with himself. Of all the places he sensed the presence of God, out here surrounded by nature and under the stars was one of the most tangible.

You mean "out here" away from religion and its incessant demands and empty promises? "Out here" to cry, to be real and embarrassed, and free to be known, accepted, and even be small?

[The Great Spirit is] a good name for God because he is a Spirit and he is Great.

Today, "Great Spirit" is too vague for me. I need a Person who knows me and loves me, who whispers that somehow this is all going to work out, that I don't have to understand, that I can let go of control, and you have a hold on me and that I am not powerful enough to make you leave. Today, that's what I need.

"Daddy?"

"Yes, honey?"

"Will I ever have to jump off a cliff?"

"No, honey. I will never ask you to jump off a cliff, never, ever, ever."

While I am grateful that you do not require religious sacrifice, I do understand that growth requires risk, so I want you to know, as terrifying as it feels to me, I am willing to jump and learn to trust your arms.

As he sat mesmerized by the fire and wrapped in its warmth, he prayed, mostly prayers of thanksgiving. He had been given so much. Blessed was probably the right word. He was content, at rest, and full of peace. Mack did not know it then, but within twenty-four hours his prayers would change drastically.

I am grateful that you don't want me seeing into the future! If I did, I would live in shadows of "impending sorrow and tragedy" and could not enjoy the "now" goodness of life. Thank you, thank you, thank you!

It is remarkable how a
seemingly insignificant action
or event can change entire lives.

Thank you for the moments we catch out of the corner of our eye. Thank you for orchestrating the ripples in places we are too blind to see. Thank you that we matter!

By now he had only one prayer left: "Dear God, please, please, please take care of my Missy. I just can't right now." Tears traced their way down his cheeks and then spilled off onto his shirt.

Sometimes I am so furious at my own impotence, my utter inability to protect and keep those I love from hurt. Please find me in my failure and fury and see past it to my heart.

Shortly after the summer that Missy vanished, The Great Sadness had draped itself around Mack's shoulders like some invisible but almost tangibly heavy quilt.

Y ea, though I walk the valley of the shadow of death." I hadn't intended to set up camp here. Please find me in my loneliness and despair. I'm having trouble finding you.

*At some point in the process, Mack
attempted to emerge from his own pain and
grief, at least with his family. They had lost
a sister and daughter, but it would be wrong
for them to lose a father and husband as well.*

Please, I need your strength, your
empowering, your determination.
I don't feel like I have anything left.
Please help me do the next right thing.

It is so easy to get sucked into the if-only game, and playing it is a short and slippery slide into despair.

Sometimes it's not the consequences of my poor choices that weigh the most heavy on my heart, it's the overwhelming accusations of regret, and I get pulled into imaginations of having done it differently. Help me embrace my true sorrow and find you there too.

Sometimes honesty can be incredibly messy.

Regardless the consequence, I want to be a truth teller, not a blamer or self-justifier. Help me be brave enough not to shade my answers in order to help or protect myself. Let my yes be yes and my no be no.

"Wait, you aren't thinking this is really from God, are you?"

"I'm not sure what to think. . . . I know it sounds crazy, but somehow I feel strangely drawn to find out for sure."

I confess to you that I would rather trust the certainty of what I think I know than the discomfort that might lead to a life I don't. And yet, I sense your invitation, to something more, to mystery, to . . .

And why the shack—the icon of his deepest pain? Certainly God would have better places to meet with him.

Thank you for loving me with a tenacity that doesn't let me avoid forever the places of deepest hurt and pain, especially the places I don't believe could ever be healed. And if I am going there, I am counting on you to go with me. Otherwise, forget it. Just sayin'.

23

It seemed that direct communication with God was something exclusively for the ancients and uncivilized. . . . Nobody wanted God in a box, just in a book.

I love that you cannot be contained in a book, or place, or song, or idea, or image. I want to hear you in all places, at all times. Please continue to heal me so that I can.

Maybe he's a really bright light, or a burning bush. I've always sort of pictured him as a really big grandpa with a long white flowing beard . . .

I know no form is possible without you. While I know I may never understand your true form, in my own being I find you in the beat of my heart, in the light of my smile, in the joy of my step, and in the touch of another. I find you most clearly in Jesus. You are closer to me than my own breath.

"I'm here, God. And you? You're nowhere to be found! You've never been around when I've needed you . . ."

I'm beginning to realize I have been expecting the wrong god to show up, the one who is a projection of my religion, culture, and deepest hurt. Help me take sides with Jesus against my own wounded imaginations and begin to believe that the untrustworthy god I hate doesn't even exist.

What should you do when you come to the door of a house, or cabin in this case, where God might be?

How often do I think that you don't know me, so I have to come to your house dressed properly and using the right words. And then I find out all you ever wanted was my heart, but that doesn't seem valuable enough, so I get dressed properly and try to find the right words . . . forgive me.

"My, my, my how I do love you!"—Papa

Thank you for being the love who sang the universe into being and does not know any other way to be.

Mack was speechless. In a few seconds this woman had breached pretty much every social propriety behind which he had so safely entrenched himself. But something in the way she looked at him and yelled his name made him equally delighted to see her too, even though he didn't have a clue who she was.

Yes, that would be me, with no clue most of the time. But I so want to be called and embraced by someone who loves me! Could this be true about you? My heart screams it must be so.

29 JANUARY

He had already been perched precariously on the precipice of emotion, and now the flooding scent and attendant memories staggered him. He could feel the warmth of tears beginning to gather behind his eyes, as if they were knocking on the door of his heart. It seemed that she saw them too.

Please keep telling me that you know me and that I can know you in a place that is deeper than all my fears. And let my own tears preach the truth to me even in ways my understanding cannot understand.

"It's okay honey, you can let it all out. . . . I know you've been hurt, and I know you are angry and confused. So, go ahead and let it out. It does a soul good to let the waters run once in a while—the healing waters."—Papa

Thank you for the gift of tears, especially for those moments when they are more than just exhaustion and longing. Thank you for the tenderness you are forming in my soul that would allow their presence and expression.

31

With every effort he could muster, he kept himself from falling back into the black hole of his emotions. "Not ready?" [Papa] responded. "That's okay, we'll do things on your terms and time."

I sometimes get a glimpse of your care and am amazed at your tender touch, the kindness of your timing, the grace of your understanding, the way you take me seriously, your invitation to participate. Sometimes I see the way you look at me, and it surprises me. It makes me grin!

There are times when you choose to believe something that would normally be considered absolutely irrational. It doesn't mean that it is actually irrational, but it surely is not rational.

I confess to you that I have an almost irresistible drive to control my life through reason and rationality, to live in my mind. Please teach me to get out of my head and into my life.

Perhaps there is super-rationality . . .
something that only makes sense if you can
see in a bigger picture of reality. Maybe that
is where faith fits in.

Often I find myself caught up and lost in the particulars, the details, and I lose sight of any bigger picture. I forget. I need some new eyes. I need to remember.

Mack stepped back again, feeling a bit overwhelmed. "Are there more of you?" he asked a little hoarsely.

The three looked at one another and laughed. Mack couldn't help but smile. "No, Mackenzie," chuckled the black woman. "We is all that you get, and believe me, we're more than enough."

Thank you for reminding me that you are more than enough, not that I believe you most of the time. It is so lonely when I start thinking that I am alone and have to be enough.

"Then," Mack struggled to ask, "which one of you is God?"

"I am," said all three in unison. Mack looked from one to the next, and even though he couldn't begin to grasp what he was seeing and hearing, he somehow believed them.

I want all of me to know All of YOU!

Mack turned and faced him, shaking his head. "Am I going crazy? Am I supposed to believe that God is a big black woman with a questionable sense of humor?"

Jesus laughed. "She's a riot! You can always count on her to throw you a curve or two. She loves surprises, and even though you might not think it, her timing is always perfect."

I want to fit you in my box, to control you, to make you do what I wish, and you keep refusing. Thank you!

... the Asian lady moved toward him again,
this time taking his face in both her hands.
Gradually and intentionally, she moved her
face closer to his and ... stopped and looked
deep into his eyes. Then she smiled and her
scents seemed to wrap themselves around him ...
Mack suddenly felt lighter than air, almost as
if he were no longer touching the ground.

At the speed of choice I want to be face to face with you. O Breath of God, free me from all to which I am tethered.

7

"Oh don't mind her . . .
She has that effect on everyone."

"I like it," he muttered, and all three burst
into more laughter, and Mack found himself
laughing along with them, not knowing
exactly why and not really caring either.

Holy Spirit, you are the life of everything good in my world. Thank you for those bits and pieces of light, those kisses of grace you send my way.

"Mackenzie, we all have things we value enough to collect, don't we? . . . I collect tears."

S ometimes I feel that my weeping goes unnoticed, that my crying does not matter, spilling like rain and disappearing into the dust of life. To know you collect my tears matters to me (Psalm 56:8).

"*That's why you're here, Mack... I want to heal the wound that has grown inside of you, and between us.*"—Papa

If you cannot reach across the distance that I have created between us, the wound that I have inflicted, then I am lost without hope. Help me believe that you are able.

"Don't go because you feel obligated. That won't get you any points around here. Go because it's what you want to do."—Papa

Obligation is all I have ever known, and now you whisper that it is *me* that you love and not my performance? Religion, though exhausting, seems safer. Please be my strength to take the risks involved in faith, to begin to trust our relationship. This is what I *want*.

"You're not supposed to do anything. You're free to do whatever you like," Jesus said.

Do you hear that sound? It is me screaming inside the box of my religion, the sound of my soul smothered by guilt and shame and the failure to be what I thought I was supposed to be. Find me, please, and set me free.

12

"God?"

*"I'm in the kitchen, Mackenzie.
Just follow my voice."*

But there are so many voices, so much static and heart-stopping noise. How do I know yours? You know I can only hear at 10 decibels, right? You are not talking to me at 9.9 and getting angry that I can't hear you, right? (Insecure Prayer #42)

He was sure his face betrayed the emotions he was battling to control, and then in a flash of a second he shoved everything back into his battered heart's closet, locking the door on the way out. If [Papa] knew his inner conflict, she showed nothing by her expression—still open, full of life, and inviting.

Hiding? Really? It is a game I play because I don't know your heart, don't believe that you are "for" me. Forgive me, I am only beginning to learn how not to think this way.

She didn't have to say it; he knew
she understood what was going
on inside of him, and somehow he
knew she cared about him more
than anyone ever had.

I am grateful to know that Someone
in this vast cosmos knows me beyond
words. Often I don't know how to put
in words who I am and how I feel. There
are times when silence speaks a thousand
pictures. Thank you for knowing me.

15

"So God listens to funk?" Mack had
never heard "funk" talked about in
any properly righteous terms.

"Now see here, Mackenzie. You don't
have to be lookin' out for me. I listen to
everything—and not just to the music
itself, but the hearts behind it."

I am finding out that the only reason I
ever find you in a "box" is because you
want to be where I am. Thank you!

"These kids ain't saying anything I haven't heard before; they are just full of vinegar and fizz. Lots of anger and, I must say, with some good reason too. They are just some of my kids, showin' and spoutin' off. I am especially fond of those boys, you know." —Papa

How could you be fond of anything not perfect, like me? That is the question of a guilt-stricken soul who has not yet awakened to your inconceivable love. You know me, where I come from, where I am headed, and how we are going to get there.

He was at a sudden loss for words and his million questions had all seemed to abandon him. So he stated the obvious. "You must know," he offered, "calling you Papa is a bit of a stretch for me."

"Oh, really?" She looked at him in mock surprise.

I was taught all my life names for you that kept you at a distance—"Father God," "Almighty," "Holy"—and then I overhear Jesus call you "Daddy" and "Papa." Please help me find a way across that chasm.

*Mack felt as if he were dangling over a
bottomless chasm and was afraid if he let any
of it out, he would lose control of everything.
He sought for safe footing … "Maybe, it's
because I've never known anyone I could
really call Papa."*

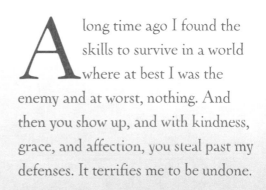

A long time ago I found the skills to survive in a world where at best I was the enemy and at worst, nothing. And then you show up, and with kindness, grace, and affection, you steal past my defenses. It terrifies me to be undone.

"If you let me, I'll be the Papa you never had."

The offer was at once inviting and at the same time repulsive. He had always wanted a Papa he could trust, but he wasn't sure he'd find it here, especially if this one couldn't even protect his Missy. A long silence hung between them. Mack was uncertain what to say, and she was in no hurry to let the moment pass easily.

What if I take the risk of trust, and you aren't who I hoped? But I know if I don't risk trust, nothing changes.

"I think it'd be easier to have this conversation if you weren't wearing a dress," he suggested and attempted a smile, as weak as it was.

"If it were easier, then I wouldn't be," [Papa] said with a slight giggle.

I want to believe that you would go out of your way . . . for me. That you know how blind and lost and deaf I am. I can't find you. Please come find me.

"If I choose to appear to you as a man or a woman, it's because I love you. For me to appear to you as a woman and suggest that you call me Papa is simply to mix metaphors, to help you keep from falling so easily back into your religious conditioning. . . . This weekend is not about reinforcing religious stereotypes."

I don't want Religion anymore; I want you! You have my permission to destroy everything in me that is keeping me from being free. (I can't believe I just prayed that!)

"Let me say for now that we knew once the Creation was broken, true fathering would be much more lacking than mothering. Don't misunderstand me, both are needed—but an emphasis on fathering is necessary because of the enormity of its absence."—Papa

So much of my faulty imaginations of you are the projections of damage caused by men in my life. Teach me to look from inside Jesus' relationship with his Papa rather than looking through my own damaged history.

23

He knew she was right, and he realized the kindness and compassion in what she was doing. Somehow, the way she had approached him had skirted his resistance to her love. It was strange, and painful, and maybe even a little bit wonderful.

Holy Spirit, please keep stealing behind our "watchful dragons" and mysteriously allowing us to suspect we may be dead wrong, and thus open us to truth more lovely than our secret dreamings.

"Honey, there's no easy answer that will take your pain away. Believe me, if I had one, I'd use it now. I have no magic wand to wave over you and make it all better."—Papa

I confess I like the idea of magic or a choice between a red or blue pill . . . instant transformation, painless if possible. There are days I hate "process" or "journey" or "adventure" and even "relationship," and yet you are whispering that I am so much more, a being wonderfully and delicately crafted, and for which there are no shortcuts.

"I often find that getting head issues out of the way first makes the heart stuff easier to work on later . . . when you're ready."—Papa

Thank you for letting me ask questions, sometimes the same ones over and over. I have been living from my head for so long that I don't know how else to do this, and now I find out it's broken too, like my heart.

"You knew I would come . . ."

"Of course I did."

"Then was I free not to come?"

"I'm not interested in prisoners . . . Just because I know . . . does that reduce your freedom to leave?"

Even in my darkness, teach me of your love, that I might choose to enjoy, to rest, to love such love and live in a real relationship from my heart. Remind me it is not about logic but relationship, a reality in which you have been eternally adept.

"Or, if you want to go just a wee bit deeper, we could talk about the nature of freedom itself. Does freedom mean that you are allowed to do whatever you want to do?"

Please set me free to live loved without an agenda. Set me free!

"I don't understand . . ."

She turned back and smiled. "I know. I didn't tell you so that you would understand right now. I told you for later. At this point, you don't even understand that freedom is an incremental process."

What in life of any lasting value is not the fruit of an "incremental process"? I forget that true relationship never has a destination.

"Only I can set you free, Mackenzie, but freedom can never be forced."—Papa

Forced love or relationship is neither. I know in the deep places of my soul that freedom comes from being loved or not at all, and yet I still want to own, to control, to force, to exchange freedom for certainty. Thank you for loving the mess that I am.

1

*"Life takes a bit of time and a
lot of relationship."*—Papa

I am such a half-hearted creature, pretending
I actually know something about life and
acting as though I know how to get there. I
am slowly, painfully learning to trust that you do
and that you are "for" me.

"Don't ever think that what my son chose to do didn't cost us dearly. Love always leaves a significant mark," [Papa] stated softly and gently. "We were there together."

Today, I celebrate that there is a "together" in you. One God, yet Three Persons. I celebrate the other-centered, self-giving fellowship and love that constitute your very eternal essence and that nothing can break your togetherness.

Gently reaching out, she took Mack's hands in hers, flour covered and all, and looking him straight in the eyes she continued, "Mackenzie, the Truth shall set you free and the Truth has a name; he's over in the woodshop right now all covered in sawdust. Everything is about him."—Papa

Thank you, Jesus, for being Truth, not a set of facts, not a dream or a place to visit, but a Person who loves us, covered in sawdust as you prepare the coffin for our great sadness. Set us free!

"At the cross? Now wait, I thought you left him—you know—'My God, my God, why hast thou forsaken me?'"

"You misunderstand the mystery there. Regardless of what he felt at that moment, I never left him. . . . Mackenzie, I never left him, and I have never left you."

You dropped into my damage, becoming my sin and crying my cry, "God, where are you?" I once believed that your Father was like many fathers, who beat their children and abandon them. Forgive me for speaking of your Father that way. I am finding out that was a lie (Psalm 22:24).

"That makes no sense to me," [Mack] snapped.

"I know it doesn't, at least not yet. Will you at least consider this: When all you can see is your pain, perhaps then you lose sight of me?"

It is undeniable that pain blinds my ability to see you. Maybe I know pain better than I know you. Maybe the certainty of its presence seems more real than the mystery of our relationship. I don't want that to be true, but sometimes it is.

"Don't forget, the story [of the cross] didn't end in his sense of forsakenness. He found his way through it to put himself completely into my hands. Oh, what a moment that was!"—Papa

Jesus, I don't have that . . . your ability to completely trust. I don't know your Papa like you do. I need you to climb inside my lack and trust on my behalf. I need to live by your faith. I will do the best I know how and add my weak voice to yours and cry, ". . . but into your hands."

7 MARCH

Papa reached for the kitchen timer, gave it a little twist, and placed it on the table in front of them. "I'm not who you think I am, Mackenzie."

I remember the first conversation about you that I read in the Hebrew Scriptures. The enemy of our hearts said that you couldn't be trusted, that you would lie to us, that you weren't good all the time, and that I was a disappointment to you. I believed him, and sometimes I still do. Please forgive me.

Mack looked at her, looked at the timer, and sighed. "I feel totally lost."

"Then let's see if we can find you in this mess."

Somewhere inside this mess, lost and even commingled with it, is the real me. Do what you must to find me, be it judgment, salvation, liberation . . . words describing the same thing, your process of discerning, finding, and separating the real me from the mess, so I can live as an authentic human being. I have nowhere else to turn.

9

"Most birds were created to fly. Being grounded for them is a limitation within their ability to fly, not the other way around. You, on the other hand, were created to be loved. So for you to live as if you were unloved is a limitation, not the other way around."

The irony is that while I believe this for children, somewhere I crossed the threshold of being created to be loved and ended valued for performance and production. I forget that I am still a child. Please remind me.

"Living unloved is like clipping a bird's wings and removing its ability to fly. Not something I want for you."

There's the rub. He didn't feel particularly loved at the moment.

Indeed, the rub. I so easily let my emotions define reality for me. I start to believe that the way I feel about myself is how you are toward me. Am I going to be embarrassed to find out how much I preferred and cherished my feelings over the truth of your love for me? You know how that makes me feel? ☺

"Mack, pain has a way of clipping our wings and keeping us from being able to fly. And if left unresolved for very long, you can almost forget that you were ever created to fly in the first place."

My regretter seems to be connected to my forgetter. I clipped my own wings. I messed things up. I made it everyone else's fault. I am so ashamed, and I don't feel worthy to even remember that I was created to fly, to be loved, to be known. Tell me again!

"I am God. I am who I am. And unlike you, my wings can't be clipped."

And yet you willingly give up flying to come and meet me where I am—lost, alone and grounded. Thank you!

"The problem is that many folks try to grasp some sense of who I am by taking the best version of themselves, projecting that to the nth degree, factoring in all the goodness they can perceive, which often isn't much, and then call that God.... it falls pitifully short of who I really am. I'm not merely the best version of you that you can think of. I am far more than that, above and beyond all that you can ask or think."

Thank you for not holding my ignorance against me.

*"Even though you can't
finally grasp me, guess what?
I still want to be known."*

Hah! I get it! Jesus is you
wanting to be known. Thank
you, thank you, thank you!

15

"This isn't Sunday School. This is a flying lesson. Mackenzie, as you might imagine, there are some advantages to being God. By nature I am completely unlimited, without bounds. I have always known fullness. I live in a state of perpetual satisfaction as my normal state of existence," she said, quite pleased. "Just one of the perks of Me being Me."

I am thrilled that I am not powerful enough to change the way that you are or are toward me. You inspire me.

*That made Mack smile. This
lady was fully enjoying herself,
all by herself, and there wasn't
an ounce of arrogance to spoil it.*

I forget that all of what makes my life so
incredible, so wonderful, penetrated by joy,
and full of beauty originated in you.

17

"But instead of scrapping the whole Creation we rolled up our sleeves and entered into the middle of the mess— that's what we have done in Jesus."

That is so the opposite of me. My tendency is to run away from messes, especially those that I had a hand in fashioning. I would rather try to start over than roll up my sleeves. Would you please help me change that in me? I want to be willing to be in the mess of life, even my own.

"When we three spoke ourself into human existence as the Son of God, we became fully human. We also chose to embrace all the limitations that this entailed. Even though we have always been present in this created universe, we now became flesh and blood. It would be like this bird, whose nature it is to fly, choosing only to walk and remain grounded. He doesn't stop being the bird, but it does alter his experience of life significantly."

I am stunned, shocked at your profound humility, that you would become one of us.

"Although by nature he is fully God, Jesus is fully human and lives as such. While never losing the innate ability to fly, he chooses moment-by-moment to remain grounded. That is why his name is Immanuel, God with us, or God with you, to be more precise."

And you never saw this as a cost or a price to pay, but an honor and a privilege; an expression of the only way you know how to love. That is the type of person I want to be.

"But what about all the miracles?
The healings? Raising people from the dead?
Doesn't that prove Jesus was God—
you know, more than human?"

"No, it proves that Jesus is truly human."

I know I have been less than human. I hurt and maim with words and expectations and judgments. Please heal me so I can be truly human and fully alive!

"Mackenzie, I can fly, but humans can't. Jesus is fully human. Although he is also fully God, he has never drawn upon his nature as God to do anything. He has only lived out of his relationship with me, living in the very same manner that I desire to be in relationship with every human being."

Jesus, I used to think you were a super hero, with secret powers, ready to pull the deity ace from your sleeve. I am so relieved that you are a true human being, participating in community. You are my hope.

"Jesus is just the first to do it to the uttermost—the first to absolutely trust my life within him, the first to believe in my love and my goodness without regard for appearance or consequence."

God, help me to absolutely trust your life within me, to believe in your love and your goodness without regard for appearance or consequence.

23

"So when he healed the blind?"

"He did so as a dependent, limited human being trusting in my life and power to be at work within him and through him. Jesus, as a human being, had no power within himself to heal anyone."

That came as a shock to Mack's religious system.

So this is about participation not performance. *Participation* is a word of relationship.

"*Only as he rested in his relationship with me, and in our communion—our co-union—could he express my heart and will into any given circumstance. So, when you look at Jesus and it appears that he's flying, he really is . . . flying. But what you are actually seeing is me; my life in him. That's how he lives and acts as a true human, how every human is designed to live—out of my life.*"

This I can "be," a helpless, dependent participant. Be my life, be my light, be my loving.

"*A bird is not defined by being grounded but by his ability to fly. Remember this, humans are not defined by their limitations, but by the intentions that I have for them; not by what they seem to be, but by everything it means to be created in my image.*"

I gave away my sense of worth, value, and importance to others, and "they" decided what it meant to be me. Then they kept changing their minds. Give me your ears, Jesus, so I can hear God tell me who I am.

"To begin with, that you can't grasp the wonder of my nature is rather a good thing. Who wants to worship a God who can be fully comprehended, eh? Not much mystery in that."

I don't want to be a grasper, trying to possess or master or control. I want to be a knower of fellowship and intimacy, of sharing in your life and feeling what your heart feels, of knowing your hands are inside mine.

"But what difference does it make that there are three of you, and you are all one God?"

"It makes all the difference in the world! We are not three gods, and we are not talking about one god with three attitudes, like a man who is a husband, father, and worker. I am one God and I am three persons, and each of the three is fully and entirely the one."

I affirm that there is only One God! Please reveal who you are to me.

"What's important is this: If I were simply One God and only One Person, then you would find yourself in this Creation without something wonderful, without something essential even. And I would be utterly other than I am."

Other-centered, self-giving love! If you were a solitary invisible singularity, then my self-centeredness would have a root and excuse. Thank you for not leaving me to wither away in my selfishness, as like you, I am wired for relationship.

"And we would be without . . . ?" Mack didn't even know how to finish the question.

"Love and relationship. All love and relationship is possible for you only because it already exists within Me, within God myself. Love is not the limitation; love is the flying. I am love."

We know love and relationship because both are already alive within you. One God who loves us the way you love one another. Stunning mystery!

He turned back to Papa, and just stared at her in wonder. She was so beautiful and astonishing, and even though he was feeling a little lost and even though The Great Sadness still attended him, he felt himself settling down somewhat into the safety of being close to her.

I want these moments when I breathe a sigh of relief, when my heart slows and I sense your tender embrace, to become the way of my life.

31

*"You do understand . . . that if I did not
have such a relationship within myself, then
I would not be capable of love at all? You
would have a god who could not love. . . .
you would have a god who, when he chose,
could only love as a limitation of his nature.
That kind of god could possibly act without
love, and that would be a disaster. And that,
is surely not me."*

I am beginning to believe that loving
is the way of your being, not just
a passing mood or fancy. I am
beginning to . . . trust.

1

With that, Papa stood up, went to the oven door, pulled out the freshly baked pie, set it on the counter and, turning around as if to present herself, said, "The God who is—the I am who I am—cannot act apart from love!"

If it is true about you, that everything you do is an expression of your nature of love, I have a lot of rethinking to do about anger, wrath, judgment, discipline, etc. Help me understand how these are expressions of your love for me.

Mack knew that what he was hearing,
as hard as it was to understand, was
something amazing and incredible.
It was as if her words were wrapping
themselves around him, embracing him
and speaking to him in ways beyond
just what he could hear.

I know that my receptors that helped me hear you and sense your presence were shattered as a child, and that you are putting them back together. Thank you for finding so many ways to help me "hear" you, such as through music, laughter, children, ocean waves, and driving rain.

3 APRIL

"Mackenzie, I know that your heart is full of pain and anger and a lot of confusion. Together, you and I, we'll get around to some of that while you're here. But I also want you to know that there is more going on than you could imagine or understand, even if I told you."

I admit there is so much I can't see or understand. I would like what I don't know to drive me deeper into trusting your character rather than questioning your activity or its seeming absence.

"As much as you are able, rest in what trust you have in me, no matter how small, okay?"

You know where I come from, why it is so difficult for me to trust anyone, let alone an invisible God, but I want what tiny flame of trust is growing to become something that fires my entire life.

"Papa?" Mack finally said in a way that felt very awkward, but he was trying.

"Yes, honey?"

"I'm so sorry that you, that Jesus, had to die."

"I know you are, and thank you. But you need to know that we aren't sorry at all. It was worth it."

Do I dare believe that perhaps, maybe, I have always been worth your kind attention and affection . . . that I matter this way to you?

*So this was God in relationship? It was
beautiful and so appealing. . . . Obviously,
what was truly important here was the love
they had for one another and the fullness it
brought them. How different this was from
the way he treated the ones he loved!*

Help me to see in the
relationships of others the
possibilities that I could
make different choices and experience

somet

mysel

"You don't play a game or color a picture with a child to show your superiority. Rather, you choose to limit yourself so as to facilitate and honor that relationship. You will even lose a competition to accomplish love. It is not about winning and losing, but about love and respect."

I confess that I have often thought of you as self-centered, proud in your supremacy and dominance, and needing the created cosmos to bow to your superiority, but Jesus, for you to be a submitting servant and kind? My universe is upended!

"Relationships are never about power, and one way to avoid the will to power is to choose to limit oneself—to serve. Humans often do this—in touching the infirm and sick, in serving the ones whose minds have left to wander, in relating to the poor, in loving the very old and the very young, or even in caring for the other who has assumed a position of power over them."

Power is about my need to control and, behind that, my insecurity. Help me see with the eyes of the other, to understand sacrifice and resurrection are sisters.

9

"*I want to have a time of devotion.*"

Jesus reached across the table and took Papa's hands in his, scars now clearly visible on his wrists. "Papa, I loved watching you today, as you made yourself fully available to take Mack's pain into yourself, and then give him space to choose his own timing. You honored him, and you honored me. To listen to you whisper love and calm into his heart was truly incredible. What a joy to watch! I love being your son."

My heart leaps in the presence of such relational and natural intimacy. I want this!

*To be in the presence of such love expressed seemed
to dislodge an inner emotional logjam, and while
he didn't understand exactly what he felt—it
was good. What was he witnessing? Something
simple, warm, intimate, genuine; this was holy.
Holiness had always been a cold and sterile
concept to Mack, but this was neither.*

I forget you were Holy before creation, before sin and damage, and that holiness celebrates your unique, one-of-a-kind, in-a-class-by-itself love that dances between and within you . . . and includes me.

Mack nodded. This presence-of-God-thing, although hard to grasp, seemed to be steadily penetrating past his mind and into his heart.

In the obscurity of my dimmed mind and broken heart, there has been a secret unknown to me, that you, Father, Son, and Spirit have already found your way into this deep darkness and are for me in a way I cannot be.

"Let's go out on the dock and look at the stars. . . . C'mon," said Jesus, interrupting Mack's thoughts. "I know you enjoy looking at stars! Want to?" He sounded just like a child full of anticipation and expectancy.

Y ou are so thrilled to share what you already know, to climb inside my "wow." Me? I want to turn what I know into a commodity that I can sell for a scrap of self-worth or security. Yuck! It seems I have a long way to go.

It almost felt like he was falling up into space, the stars racing toward him as if to embrace him. He lifted his hands imagining that he could reach out and pluck diamonds, one by one, off of a velvet-black sky.

"Wow!" he whispered.

Jesus, you have placed your Holy Presents all around to startle and surprise me. May they even for a moment interrupt my smallness and pull me into the vastness of your creativity.

Mack was not sure how to describe what he felt, but as they continued to lie in silence, gazing into the celestial display, watching and listening, he knew in his heart that this too was holy. As they both watched in awestruck wonder, shooting stars would occasionally blaze a brief trail across the night blackness causing one or the other to exclaim, "Did you see that? Awesome!"

Thank you for unexpected bits of delight that fill me with a sense of hope.

15

"Incredible!" whispered Jesus, his head near Mack's in the darkness. "I never get tired of this."

"Even though you created it?" Mack asked.

"I created it as the Word, before the Word became flesh. So even though I created this, I see it now as a human. And I must say, it is impressive."

Such encouragement to know that delighting in the creativity of my spirit, soul, and body is both utterly human and wholly divine.

After a particularly long silence, Mack spoke. "I feel more comfortable around you. You seem so different than the other two.... More real, or tangible.... It's like I've always known you."

You found a chasm in my understanding, an abyss within my heart, and without a single condemnation you chose to be the bridge across. Thank you! I have no other words.

17

*"Since I am human we have much in common
to begin with. . . . I am the best way any
human can relate to Papa or Sarayu. To see
me is to see them. The love you sense from me
is no different from how they love you."*

Forgive me for believing
you had come to rescue
me from Papa God.

"... Sarayu, is she the Holy Spirit?"

"Yes. She is Creativity; she is Action; she is the Breathing of Life; she is much more. She is my Spirit."

"And her name, Sarayu?"

"That is a simple name from one of our human languages. It means 'Wind,' a common wind actually. She loves that name."

You are the common wind who catches me by surprise, the water that quenches my eternal thirst, the hidden fountain from whom flows thought, music, creativity, and freedom. Come, fill me up, and please never stop.

"And the name Papa mentioned, Elo . . . El . . ."

"Elousia," the voice spoke reverently from the dark next to him. "That is a wonderful name. El is my name as Creator God, but ousia is 'being' or 'that which is truly real,' so the name means the Creator God who is truly real and the ground of all being. Now that is also a beautiful name."

What if the way of your being and living and fellowship is written into the fabric of the universe, the ground of our existence and destiny, and what if that is love?

Mack lay there a few seconds and realized that as much as he thought he knew Jesus, perhaps he didn't . . . not really. Maybe what he knew was an icon, an ideal, an image through which he tried to grasp a sense of spirituality, but not a real person.

Having an idea of you or a theology about you is easier for me to manage and less messy than actually knowing you. Relationship is interference and mystery. Even while I hate it, I want it with every fiber of my being.

"You said if I really know you it wouldn't matter what you looked like . . . [Why is that?]"

"It is quite simple really. Being always transcends appearance—that which only seems to be. Once you begin to know the being behind the very pretty or very ugly face, as determined by your bias, the surface appearances fade away until they simply no longer matter."

I am so guilty of judging by first and outward appearance and impression. Teach me how to see the way you see—the true, the real, the deep, the transcendent that spills through the ordinary.

"That's why Elousia is such a wonderful name. God, who is the ground of all being, dwells in, around, and through all things—ultimately emerging as the real—and any appearances that mask that reality will fall away."

I can fool myself and others. I can spin, quote, and look the part, but the day will come when I will know that you know that I know that you know. All pretense will be undone, and there will be nowhere to hide. All appearances, illusions, delusions, and cons will vanish, and I will at last know as I am known—loved forever.

"But don't think that just because I'm not visible, our relationship has to be less real. It will be different, but perhaps even more real. . . . My purpose from the beginning was to live in you and you in me."

Jesus, you are so imbedded into my life and living; you are so close to me—my burdens, insights, joys, and pains—that I cannot see you, not yet.

"Wait, wait. Wait a minute. How can that happen? If you're still fully human, how can you be inside me?"

"Astounding, isn't it? It's Papa's miracle. It is the power of Sarayu, my Spirit, the Spirit of God who restores the union that was lost so long ago. Me? I choose to live moment by moment fully human. I am fully God, but I am human to the core. Like I said, it's Papa's miracle."

You are a mystery. From time to time I get glimpses, and I am amazed!

25

"The human, formed out of the physical material Creation, can once more be fully indwelt by spiritual life, my life. It requires that a very real dynamic and active union exists."

I confess . . . again . . . that sometimes I would rather you were an ideology or doctrine than personal and relational; it has been easier to be right than it ever has to trust and change.

In the silence that followed, Mack simply lay still, allowing the immensity of space and scattered light to dwarf him, letting his perceptions be captured by starlight and the thought that everything was about him ... about the human race ... that all this was all for us.

I want to be still, to be captured in the silence, embraced in the wonder, to believe that you are now and always have been "for" us.

After what seemed like a long time, it was Jesus who broke into the quiet.

"I'll never get tired of looking at this. The wonder of it all—the wastefulness of Creation, as one of our brothers has called it. So elegant, so full of longing and beauty even now."

We are on this tiny planet, barely a speck in the vastness of this universe, and you are not only mindful of us, but we are the center of your affection. You are extravagant in your grace, beautifully wasteful in your creativity.

"*You know,*" *Mack responded, suddenly struck anew by the absurdity of his situation; where he was, the person next to him. "Sometimes you sound so, I mean, here I am lying next to God Almighty and, you really sound, so . . .*"

"*Human?*" *Jesus offered. "But ugly." And with that he began to chuckle . . .*

To think that you have chosen to forever be one with us in our humanity. Very God of very God, with calloused hands and a sense of humor.

It was infectious, and Mack found himself swept along, from somewhere deep inside. He had not laughed from down there in a long time. Jesus reached over and hugged him, shaking from his own spasms of mirth, and Mack felt more clean and alive and well than he had since . . . well, he couldn't remember since when.

What a gift, to laugh. There is nothing that sings to me of relationship quite like it. In those moments I feel like a well-loved child.

"Jesus?" he whispered as his voice choked. "I feel so lost."

A hand reached out and squeezed his and didn't let go. "I know, Mack. But it's not true. I am with you, and I'm not lost."

Thank you for not minimizing my feelings or making me feel ashamed for having them. Thank you for not letting go even when I don't know how to hold on. Thank you for just . . . being with me. You know how lost I feel sometimes. Thank you!

1 MAY

Those who have never flown this way might think those who believe they do rather daft, but secretly they are probably at least a little envious. He hadn't had a flying dream in years, not since The Great Sadness had descended, but tonight Mack flew high into the starlit night . . .

Lift my spirit, hold my hand, and teach me to soar even in the darkness of my world. Today, I give you my heartaches.

"This can't really be happening," Mack grunted . . . Papa—whoever she was—made him nervous and he had no idea what to make of Sarayu. He admitted to himself that he liked Jesus a lot, but he seemed the least godlike of the three.

Mack shook his head, dumbfounded. What was going on here? Who were they really and what did they want from him? Whatever it was, he was sure he didn't have it to give.

At times I don't even know how to give you my brokenness, my confusion. I am trusting that you can find your way to me.

3

*"How were your dreams last night?
Dreams are sometimes important, you
know. They can be a way of openin' up the
window and lettin' the bad air out."*

Please guide me with the wisdom of a discerning mind, and give me eyes to see and a heart open to what you are revealing to me in my most vulnerable places.

"*Is he your favorite?*"

"*Mackenzie, I have no favorites; I am just especially fond of him.*"

To say you love me is about you. To say you are especially fond of me is about me. Dare I believe that? That you who know me so completely would still be fond of me?

"*You seem to be especially fond of a lot of people,*" *Mack observed with a suspicious look. "Are there any who you are not especially fond of?"*

She lifted her head and rolled her eyes as if she were mentally going through the catalog of every being ever created. "Nope, I haven't been able to find any. Guess that's jes' the way I is."

I am starting to believe that I don't have the power to change your affection toward me. It's rocking my world!

6

Mack was interested. "Do you ever get mad at any of them?"

"Sho 'nuff! What parent doesn't? There is a lot to be mad about in the mess my kids have made and in the mess they're in. I don't like a lot of choices they make, but that anger—especially for me—is an expression of love all the same. I love the ones I am angry with just as much as those I'm not."

Help me be the right kind of angry— angry that is an expression of love!

"I understand how disorienting all this must be for you, Mack. But the only one pretending here is you. I am what I am. I'm not trying to fit anyone's bill."

It was you who put the longing for authenticity so deep within me. I don't know how to get from disintegrated to become "I am who I am." Please hear and answer my cry.

"I'm not asking you to believe anything, but I will tell you that you're going to find this day a lot easier if you simply accept what is, instead of trying to fit it into your preconceived notions."

I live largely inside my assumptions, expectations, and preconceptions. It's not working very well. Holy Spirit, I need a new prescription for the way I "see."

At that, Papa stopped her preparations and turned toward Mack. He could see a deep sadness in her eyes. "I am not who you think I am, Mackenzie."

I know I have created an image of you from my own damaged imagination. I thought it would give me control and I would feel safe, but I doomed myself to a life, a kingdom, and a salvation of my own making. I want to know you for who you are.

"I don't need to punish people for sin. Sin is its own punishment, devouring you from the inside. It's not my purpose to punish it; it's my joy to cure it." —Papa

I am beginning to understand that it goes deeper, that it is your intention to utterly destroy sin, because it is hurting and imprisoning the very ones you love. Please be the fire that burns from me everything that keeps me from being free.

11

"I don't understand . . ."

"You're right. You don't," she said with a smile still sad around its edges. "But then again, we're not done yet."

I forget that a few years ago I thought my opinion was the right one, and look how much I have changed. Help me remember that this is not a destination, but more change and growth is coming.

Mack was spellbound watching and listening as Papa joined in the conversation Jesus and Sarayu were having. He never had seen three people share with such simplicity and beauty. Each seemed more aware of the others than of themself.

I desire my relationships to be like yours, with not a single hint of shadow, no hiding, no fear, no ambition, no greed, no self-protection, no agenda, no expectation, and no demand.

"Well, I know that you are one and all, and that there are three of you. But you respond with such graciousness to each other. Isn't one of you more the boss than the other two?"

The three looked at one another as if they had never thought of such a question.

I keep trying to twist your being and relationship into ones that I am familiar with, patterns of power and control, and you keep messing me up with servanthood and submission.

14

"*Mackenzie, we have no concept of final authority among us, only unity. We are in a circle of relationship, not a chain of command or 'great chain of being' as your ancestors termed it. What you're seeing here is relationship without any overlay of power. We don't need power over the other because we are always looking out for the best.*"

And me? I keep trying to figure out where in the chain I belong, so at least I can feel superior to someone else. Makes me sick at heart.

"Humans are so lost and damaged that to you it is almost incomprehensible that people could work or live together without someone being in charge."

"It's one reason why experiencing true relationship is so difficult for you."

But I want it to be someone else's fault. I don't want to own my mistakes and choices. I want someone to tell me what to do. I would rather sit clothed and smug in someone's prison than naked and uncertain in my own freedom. . . . Please destroy whatever it is that would make me settle for such bondage.

16

"Once you have a hierarchy you need rules to protect and administer it, and then you need law and enforcement of the rules, and you end up with some kind of chain of command or a system of order that destroys relationship rather than promotes it. You rarely see or experience relationship apart from power. Hierarchy imposes laws and rules and you end up missing the wonder of relationship that we intended for you."

You know that this is all we know. We are blind and lost. Please come find us.

17 MAY

"Well," said Mack sarcastically . . .
"We sure seem to have adapted pretty well to it."

Sarayu was quick to reply, "Don't confuse
adaptation for intention, or seduction for reality."

Please give me wisdom to discern when change is seduction leading to bondage and not transformation leading to freedom.

"When you chose independence over relationship, you became a danger to each other. Others became objects to be manipulated or managed for your own happiness. Authority, as you usually think of it, is merely the excuse the strong use to make others conform to what they want."

If we don't have hierarchy or relationships of power, what happens to security? Trust? You want me to trust?

19

"We carefully respect your choices, so we work within your systems even while we seek to free you from them," Papa continued. "Creation has been taken down a very different path than we desired."

Jesus, teach me to participate with you in this—respecting the choices of the other, entering into their world, and without coercion and power being present to serve as an agent of freedom.

"In your world the value of the individual is constantly weighed against the survival of the system, whether political, economic, social, or religious—any system actually. First one person, and then a few, and finally even many are easily sacrificed for the good and ongoing existence of that system."

. . . and you would leave the ninety-nine to go and find the one.

"In one form or another this lies behind every struggle for power, every prejudice, every war, and every abuse of relationship. The 'will to power and independence' has become so ubiquitous that it is now considered normal."

What if what we think is normal is wrong, dead wrong?

"As the crowning glory of Creation, you were made in our image, unencumbered by structure and free to simply 'be' in a relationship with me and one another."

That Garden was so long ago. We barely have a remembrance, and yet it survives in our deepest longings. I want that, for me, for the ones I love, for my enemies, for all humanity, for the entire cosmos.

"If you truly learned to regard each other's concerns as significant as your own, there would be no need for hierarchy."

. . . and the world as I know it, and what I thought my place was in it, would crumble. May I just say, this scares me and also gives me hope!

"You humans are so lost and damaged that to you it is almost incomprehensible that relationship could exist apart from hierarchy. So you think that God must relate inside a hierarchy like you do. But we do not."

If this is true, what would that say about all of our religious systems, all the "job security" and economics of our religious administrations, all the scrambling and posturing for religious superiority? What would it be like to find our place apart from power and control?

"We (the Father, Son, and Holy Spirit) won't use you. We want to share with you the love and joy and freedom and light that we already know within ourself."

To be used by another is to be disregarded. To be included is to be supremely honored. Thank you for not being a "user" but including us all.

"We created you, the human, to be in face-to-face relationship with us, to join our circle of love. As difficult as it will be for you to understand, everything that has taken place is occurring exactly according to this purpose, without violating choice or will."

I once believed that you were an abuser, for my own good, of course. I now believe that is a lie.

27

"There are millions of reasons to allow
pain and hurt and suffering rather than
to eradicate them, but most of those
reasons can only be understood within
each person's story."

Holy Spirit, you are a redeeming genius,
always working to transform my sorrow
and pain into sacraments of everlasting
love. I am grateful that there is no universal script.

"I am not evil. You are the ones who embrace fear and pain and power and rights so readily in your relationships. But your choices are also not stronger than my purposes, and I will use every choice you make for the ultimate good and the most loving outcome."

This is my hope; that I am neither strong enough to change your character nor powerful enough to alter your purposes, and that you are good, all the time.

"Broken humans center their lives around things that seem good to them, but that will neither fill them nor free them. They are addicted to power or the illusion of security that power offers."

What an anguishing sense of loss and emptiness when we finally achieve that which we thought would fill us and find that it did not. Perhaps we prefer retaining the illusions of its offer rather than obtain it and find out. How sad and desperate!

*"If you could only see how all of this ends
and what we will achieve without the
violation of one human will—then you
would understand. One day you will."*

I want your loving to be bigger than my best attempts, a loving that sings my deepest desire and longing, and I want your kind of loving to win . . . everything! My heart yearns for "one day."

"If you knew I was good and that everything—
the means, the ends, and all the processes of
individual lives—is all covered by my goodness,
then while you might not always understand
what I am doing, you would trust me."

So this is what we always come back to . . . trust.
And trust always comes back to the question of
your character, your goodness. Could I just go
back to trying to obey a list of rules? No? Thank you!
Somewhere inside I know it is trust that I truly want,
just don't know how to get from here to there.

1 JUNE

"You really don't understand yet. You try to make sense of the world in which you live based on a very small and incomplete picture of reality. It is like looking at a parade through the tiny knothole of hurt, pain, self-centeredness, and power, and believing you are on your own and insignificant. All of these contain powerful lies."

Please help me to see the lies that have me so locked away from real life, even the lies I think are precious.

"You cannot produce trust just like you cannot 'do' humility. It either is or is not. Trust is the fruit of a relationship in which you know you are loved."

I am discovering that trusting you is both complex and simple. Complex because my mind screams "no" at anything that feels illogical or risky. Simple because once I find myself willing to ignore that scream and believe you actually love me, trusting seems the most natural thing to do.

3

"I am good, and I desire only what is best for you. You cannot find that through guilt or condemnation or coercion, only through a relationship of love. And I do love you."

Thank you for loving me. Please allow our relationship to flow in me and through me. Silence the voices of guilt. Reverse the years of condemnation. Free me from the religious coercion I received . . . and gave.

*"I just want you to be with me
and discover that our relationship
is not about performance or you
having to please me."*

I can't imagine any relationship not being
about performance . . . of course, unless I
am loved and accepted as I am. Learning to
trust you rather than trying to please you . . .

"One last comment," he added, turning back. *"I just can't imagine any final outcome that would justify all this."*

"Mackenzie." Papa rose out of her chair and walked around the table to give him a big squeeze. *"We're not justifying it. We are redeeming it."*

I suppose that the way I justify myself is actually my religion. Please teach me to live more like you, not justifying myself but participating in real change and redemption.

Mack followed Sarayu as best he could . . . To walk behind such a being was like tracking a sunbeam. Light seemed to radiate through her and then reflect her presence in multiple places at once. Her nature was rather ethereal, full of dynamic shades and hues of color and motion. "No wonder so many people are a little unnerved at relating to her," Mack thought. "She obviously is not a being who is predictable."

Dear Holy Spirit, thank you for your unpredictability! Unnerving and grace-full.

"*From above it's a fractal. . . . something considered simple and orderly that is actually composed of repeated patterns no matter how magnified. A fractal is almost infinitely complex. I love fractals. I put them everywhere.*"—*Sarayu*

I am surrounded by your intricate complexity and elegance, and to most of it, I am blind and uncomprehending. Touch my eyes, please!

8

"*Looks like a mess to me,*" *muttered Mack under his breath.*

Sarayu stopped and turned to Mack, her face glorious. "Mack! Thank you! What a wonderful compliment!" She looked around at the garden. "That is exactly what this is—a mess. But," she looked back at Mack and beamed, "it's still a fractal, too."

I am the mess! Could it be that you are at home here, in this mess, in me?

9 JUNE

"Oh Mackenzie, if only you knew. It's not the work, but the purpose that makes it special. And," she smiled at him, "it's the only kind I do."

Help me not lose the sense of purpose in even the most ordinary parts of life—the mundane, the required, the routine, the usual.

"So you're saying that you ..."

"... created everything that actually exists, including what you consider the bad stuff," Sarayu completed his sentence. *"But when I created it, it was only Good, because that is just the way I am."*

Some day you are going to have to explain to me mosquitoes, gnats, yellow jackets, and poison oak ...

11

"You humans, so little in your own eyes. You are truly blind to your own place in the Creation. Having chosen the ravaged path of independence, you don't even comprehend that you are dragging the entire Creation along with you. So very sad, but it won't be this way forever."

My prayer today is that we find a way to lift our eyes from the mess we have made and dare begin to love ourselves as your incredible creation, profound in purpose and included in your majesty!

"There are times when it is safe to touch, and times when precautions must be taken. That is the wonder and adventure of exploration, a piece of what you call science—to discern and discover what we have hidden for you to find."

Teach me, please, how to explore from inside the freedom of relationship and community, and not as an independent cell that becomes a danger to its own self and others.

*"Why do children love to hide and seek?
Ask any person who has a passion to explore
and discover and create. The choice to hide
so many wonders from you is an act of love
that is a gift inside the process of life."*

Thank you, thank you, thank you for this gift—to uncover and examine and create and imagine, to wonder and perceive, for the "aha" and the thrill of finding, for countless treasures hidden all around us and the journey to discovering them.

*"Freedom involves trust and obedience
inside a relationship of love."*

I thought freedom was independence. I was
wrong. I want to be truly free! I want to learn
how to trust! I want to know you love me!

"So why create poisonous plants at all?"
Mack queried.

"Your question presumes that poison is bad; that such creations have no purpose. Many of these so-called bad plants, like this one, contain incredible properties for healing or are necessary for some of the most magnificent wonders when combined with something else."

I confess my capacity for abusing your creation and wrapping such exploitation in self-justifying language. I confess I want to commoditize your beauty for my own self-centered "good." Please change this in me.

"Humans have a great capacity for declaring something good or evil, without truly knowing."

Because of my own insecurity, I have never been comfortable with not knowing. So I have projected an aura of knowing, of brilliance, of intelligence to cover my own nakedness. Today, I would like to declare, "I don't know . . . and I am becoming more at ease with this."

17 JUNE

*"To prepare this ground, we must dig
up the roots of all the wonderful growth
that was here. It is hard work, but well
worth it. If the roots are not here, then
they cannot do what comes naturally
and harm the seed we will plant."*

Thank you for respecting me
enough not to heal me apart
from my own participation.
"We" must dig up the roots.

"I can see now," confessed Mack, "that I spend most of my time and energy trying to acquire what I have determined to be good, whether it's financial security or health or retirement or whatever. And I spend a huge amount of energy and worry fearing what I've determined to be evil."

How embarrassing it will be, in a good way, when in the light I finally see how much I invested in wrong things.

*"Rumors of glory are often hidden inside
of what many consider myths and tales."*

I love that hidden inside our children's
tales and stories are deepest longings . . .
that we all want evil to be vanquished, to
be woken from our darkened sleep, rescued
by the King's Son, and live happily ever after.

"When something happens to you, how do you determine whether it is good or evil?"

Mack thought for a moment before answering. "... I guess I would say that something is good when I like it—when it makes me feel good or gives me a sense of security. Conversely, I'd call something evil that causes me pain or costs me something I want. ... All seems quite self-serving and self-centered, I suppose."

Unless you climb into my heart and mind, I will be lost inside this self-serving and self-centered existence. You are my hope ... to change.

"Then it is you who determines good and evil. You become the judge. And to make things more confusing, that which you determine to be good will change over time and circumstance. And then beyond that and even worse, there are billions of you each determining what is good and what is evil."

There is a place where arguments cease, where our theories, ideas, and judgments lose all meaning. We will each be discerned, and that will be our salvation.

"So when your good and evil clashes with your neighbor's, fights and arguments ensue and even wars break out."

I am exhausted and disheartened by our wars, the brutality in our words, and the prejudice that finds a home in our darkened hearts. Today, I wonder why you put up with us, why you bother. But then I remember that you have not only joined us but become one with us, so that in you we might find another way.

"If there is no reality of good that is absolute, then you have lost any basis for judging. It is just language, and one might as well exchange the word good for the word evil."

It sounds ridiculous to even admit it, but I tend to make myself the measure of all things, as if I was the "good" absolute. It hasn't worked out very well. I don't want to judge anymore.

"It allows you to play God in your independence. That's why part of you prefers not to see me. And you don't need me at all to create your list of good and evil. But you do need me if you have any desire to stop such an insane lust for independence."

I am beginning to suspect that our religions are designed to keep you at a distance, under control, so that we can continue to hide from you, even while they make us feel that we are true worshipers.

25 JUNE

"So is there a way to fix it?" asked Mack.

"You must give up your right to decide what is good and evil on your own terms. That is a hard pill to swallow; choosing to only live in me. To do that you must know me enough to trust me and learn to rest in my inherent goodness."

Holy Spirit, I do not want to see things the way that I see them anymore. Give me Jesus' eyes, Papa's heart, and your love.

"*Mackenzie, evil is a word we use to describe the absence of Good, just as we use the word darkness to describe the absence of Light or death to describe the absence of Life. Both evil and darkness can only be understood in relation to Light and Good; they do not have any actual existence. I am Light and I am Good. I am Love and there is no darkness in me. Light and Good actually exist. So, removing yourself from me will plunge you into darkness. Declaring independence will result in evil because apart from me, you can only draw upon yourself. That is death because you have separated yourself from me: Life.*"

Do what you must so I may share your life.

27

"Didn't Missy have a right to be protected?"

"No, Mack. A child is protected because she is loved, not because she has a right to be protected."

Teach me to love inside your loving, to remember that every person was once a child and that every person is loved, whether they know it or not.

"Rights are where survivors go, so that they won't have to work out relationships."

Help me to not hide behind my rights, but risk in relating to what others see. You know I am a survivor and that relationships are my largest wound and scare me. I am more used to presenting my rights than my heart. Help me change!

Mack was getting frustrated. He spoke louder, "But, don't I have the right to . . ."

"To complete a sentence without being interrupted? No, you don't. Not in reality. But as long as you think you do, you will surely get ticked off when someone cuts you off, even if it is God."

In the dark I have defined and divided, declared and judged, so to have the illusion of control, and I have missed the myriad of combinations and had to live inside my own conclusions. I have been a right instead of a human.

"Mackenzie, Jesus didn't hold on to any rights; he willingly became a servant and lives out of his relationship to Papa. He gave up everything, so that by his dependent life he opened a door that would allow you to live free enough to give up your rights."

If you are not real, if you are not good, I won't be able to take the risk and let go of my rights. Live in me, Jesus, the one who makes himself humble, who serves.

"Mackenzie, you are such a delight! Thank you for all your hard work."

"I didn't do that much, really," he apologized. "I mean look at this mess." His gaze moved over the garden that surrounded them. "But this is really beautiful, and full of you, Sarayu. Even though it seems like lots of work still needs to be done, I feel strangely at home and comfortable here."

I get so bewildered by my own perspective. You have a way of seeing beauty that resides in what I consider loss. Heal my eyes!

2

"And well you should, Mackenzie, because this garden is your soul. This mess is you! Together, you and I, we have been working with a purpose in your heart. And it is wild and beautiful and perfectly in process. To you it seems like a mess, but to me, I see a perfect pattern emerging and growing and alive—a living fractal."

My soul? Could it be that you have already found your way into the garden of my soul?

The impact of her words almost crumbled all of Mack's reserve. He looked again at their garden—his garden—and it really was a mess, but incredible and wonderful at the same time. And beyond that, Papa was here and Sarayu loved the mess. It was almost too much to comprehend and once again his carefully guarded emotions threatened to spill over.

This is difficult for me, that you know me so completely and are not embarrassed or ashamed of dwelling here with me, in me.

"Now," Jesus folded his arms, "we both know that you are a very capable swimmer, once a lifeguard if I remember right. And the water is cold. And it's deep. But I'm not talking about swimming. I want to walk across with you."

With me? A declaration of dependence? I want to walk across too . . . with you!

"C'mon, Mack. If Peter can do it . . ."

Thank you for the "great cloud" that witness to your goodness and grace, who encourage me in the next step, no matter how impossible it looks or feels.

"Peter had the same problem:
How to get out of the boat."

Sometimes you make me grin!
Confidence is high, but I'm still not
sure how to get out of this boat.

"You imagine. Such a powerful ability, the imagination! That power alone makes you so like us. But without wisdom, imagination is a cruel taskmaster."

Imagination is a bittersweet gift. I both love and abhor where it takes me. You are the origin of creative imagination, so please teach me how to treasure but steer this wonder.

8

"*Do you think humans were designed to live in the present or the past or the future?*"

"*Well, I think the most obvious answer is that we were designed to live in the present.*"

"*Relax, Mack; this is not a test, it's a conversation. You are exactly correct, by the way.*"

Religion has conditioned me to always treat every encounter with you as a test, a pass/fail that I will probably fail. I forget that you are relationship, not religion.

"But now tell me, where do you spend most of your time in your mind, in your imagination, in the present, in the past, or in the future?"

"I suppose I would have to say that I spend very little time in the present. For me, I spend a big piece in the past, but most of the rest of the time, I am trying to figure out the future."

The present is raw, real, alive, and scary, commanding my attention. I see how you have been with me, but only in the present can I actually be with you.

"When I dwell with you, I do so in the present—I live in the present. Not the past, although much can be remembered and learned by looking back, but only for a visit, not an extended stay. And for sure, I do not dwell in the future you visualize or imagine."

Please, will you even meet me when I am lost in my own imaginations? Thank you!

11 JULY

"Mack, do you realize that your imagination of the future, which is almost always dictated by fear of some kind, rarely, if ever, pictures me there with you?"

This would make sense, since you don't live in anything that is not real. I confess that sometimes my fearful imaginations are more real to me than you are.

"*Why do I do that?*" *asked Mack.*

"*It is your desperate attempt to get some control over something you can't.*"

I am so all about control. Sometimes I want to control people rather than have a relationship with them or to control circumstances rather than trust you. I often want certainty more than faith. You knew this going in, right? (Insecure Prayer #213)

13

"It is impossible for you to take power of the future because it isn't even real, nor will it ever be real. You try and play God, imagining the evil that you fear becoming a reality, and then you try and make plans and contingencies to avoid what you fear."

Help me stop spending today's grace on imaginations, especially those of the future, that aren't even real.

"So why do I have so much fear in my life?"

"Because you don't believe. You don't know that we love you."

You're right, I don't. I am an unbeliever when it comes to your love for me. Help my unbelief.

15 JULY

"The person who lives by their fears will not find freedom in my life. I am not talking about rational fears regarding legitimate dangers, but imagined fears. . . . To the degree that those fears have a place in your life, you neither believe that I am good nor know deep in your heart that I love you."

So today, as best I know how, I believe you love me.

"I have so far to go."

"Only about a foot, it looks to me," laughed Jesus.

It was all he needed and Mack stepped off the dock.

Help me understand what is my next step, what is right in front of me, and be my courage to step off of what appears to be solid into what seems to be impossible.

Walking on the water with Jesus seemed like the most natural way to cross a lake, and Mack was grinning ear to ear just thinking about what he was doing.

"This is utterly ridiculous and impossible, you know," he finally exclaimed.

"Of course," assented Jesus, grinning back at him.

As much as it terrifies me, I have this sense that I was created for the impossible, the ridiculous and improbable. I love that! Did I mention it terrifies me?

"*You do great work!*" *he said softly.*

"*Thank you, Mack, and you've seen so little. For now most of what exists in the universe will only be seen and enjoyed by me, like special canvasses in the back of an artist's studio, but one day . . . And can you imagine this scene if the earth was not at war, striving so hard just to survive?*"

"Things which eye has not seen and ear has not heard, and which have not entered the heart of a human being, all that you have prepared for those whom you love" (1 Corinthians 2:9).

"Our earth is like a child who has grown up without parents, having no one to guide and direct her." As Jesus spoke, his voice intensified in subdued anguish. "Some have attempted to help her but most have simply tried to use her. Humans, who have been given the task to lovingly steer the world, instead plunder her with no consideration, other than their immediate needs. And they give little thought for their own children who will inherit their lack of love. So they use her and abuse her with little consideration and then when she shudders or blows her breath, they are offended and raise their fist at God."

Forgive us! We don't know what we are doing.

"You must care deeply about the Creation," smiled Mack.

"Well, this blue-green ball in black space belongs to me," Jesus stated emphatically.

Jesus, everything on this planet, indeed everything in this cosmos exists for, by, through, and is sustained in you. Teach us to live within your life and in this place with appropriate reverence and respect.

21

"So why don't you fix it?" Mack asked. "The earth, I mean."

"Because we gave it to you."

"Can't you take it back?"

"Of course we could, but then the story would end before it was consummated."

Thank you for pouring out your Holy Spirit on "all" flesh, so that together we might learn what it means to love you, love ourselves, love one another, and love the creation.

"Have you noticed that even though you call me Lord and King, I have never really acted in that capacity with you? I've never taken control of your choices or forced you to do anything, even when what you were about to do was destructive or hurtful to yourself and others."

If I was Lord and King . . . I would probably be the only one left. Thank you for not becoming an abuser, even if it was "for my own good."

"To force my will on you," Jesus replied, "is exactly what love does not do. Genuine relationships are marked by submission even when your choices are not helpful or healthy."

The closest reflection I have seen of your kind of loving is the love of a parent for their child. I couldn't understand until I had my own.

"That's the beauty you see in my relationship with Abba and Sarayu. We are indeed submitted to one another and have always been so and always will be."

Something deep within me shouts that this must be true, for without this other-centered, self-giving way of loving, there is nothing for me within which to be included.

"Submission is not about authority and it is not obedience; it is all about relationships of love and respect. In fact we are submitted to you in the same way."

The God of the universe, submitting to me, washing my feet? Staggered and speechless!

*"Because we want you to join us in
our circle of relationship. I don't want
slaves to my will; I want brothers and
sisters who will share life with me."*

I am beginning to think that Religion
is my drive to win your affection and
approval because I don't know you
have already included me in the very life
of Father, Son, and Holy Spirit.

"When I am your life, submission is the most natural expression of my character and nature, and it will be the most natural expression of your new nature within relationships."

You're not mad at me, are you, for not being farther down this road than I currently am? (Insecure Prayer #81)

"The world is broken because in Eden you abandoned relationship with us to assert your own independence. Most men have expressed it by turning to the work of their hands and the sweat of their brow to find their identity, value, and security. By choosing to declare what's good and evil you seek to determine your own destiny. It was this turning that has caused so much pain."

My choice of independence has been the root of much of the damage in my world. For so long it is all I knew. Please continue to heal my heart.

"It's so simple, but never easy for you. By re-turning. By turning back to me. By giving up your ways of power and manipulation and just come back to me."

Not easy! There are so many shadows in my heart and habits in my ways. My default settings need reconfiguring, and my mind needs to be converted, and the more I walk with Jesus the more I realize I don't. Thankfully, you are still able to strike a straight line with a crooked stick.

"Women . . . find it difficult to turn from a man and stop demanding that he meets their needs . . . and return to me. Men . . . find it very hard to turn from the works of their hands . . . and return to me."

That is what I want, in the deepest places of my wanting, to re-turn, to come home. And yet I fight it. I am ashamed and afraid the prodigal son was a onetime event. Help me take the risk.

"Mack, don't you see how filling roles is the opposite of relationship? We want male and female to be counterparts, face-to-face equals, each unique and different, distinctive in gender but complementary, and each empowered uniquely by Sarayu from whom all true power and authority originates."

Playing a role is safer, but you lose yourself in the process and then have this gnawing grief that you live an unauthentic life. I don't want that. I want more!

"Remember, I am not about performance and fitting into man-made structures; I am about being. As you grow in relationship with me, what you do will simply reflect who you really are."

There is a true me lost in the darkness of who I think I am. Jesus, please help me take sides with you against the lies that have grown out of my own damage.

2

*"We created a circle of relationship,
like our own, but for humans. She,
out of him, and now all the males,
including me, birthed through her, and
all originating, or birthed, from God."*

I have been trained to view independence as
strength and relationship as weakness, and yet
everything I am discovering about you is an
invitation deeper into relationship and dependence.
I am resisting because I am afraid, ironic as that is.

"*Exactly right, Mack.*" *Jesus looked at him and grinned.* "*Our desire was to create a being that had a fully equal and powerful counterpart, the male and the female. But your independence with its quest for power and fulfillment actually destroys the relationship your heart longs for.*"

And all along I thought it was "her" fault.

"Mack, just like love, submission is not something that you can do, especially not on your own. Apart from my life inside of you, you can't submit to Nan, or your children, or anyone else in your life, including Papa."

Again, I want to believe that I can do this on my own and in my own power, and all I end up with is a new set of expectations that I disappoint. Jesus, please crawl inside my independent insanity and wed your heart and its ability to submit to my broken one.

5

"Seriously, my life was not meant to be an example to copy. Being my follower is not trying to 'be like Jesus,' it means for your independence to be killed."

Please help me understand in the real-ness of life that the death of my independence is not another abandonment, but an invitation to participate.

"I came to give you life, real life, my life.
We will come and live our life inside of
you, so that you may begin to see with our
eyes and hear with our ears, and touch
with our hands, and think like we do."

How many times I crashed and burned under the stress of trying to get it right, only to discover that the "right" I was chasing was a constantly changing chimera. Thank you for sharing your nature with me so I can live from the inside out rather than outside in.

*He desperately wanted to back out into the
light, but in the end he believed that Jesus
would not have sent him in here without a
good purpose. He pressed in farther.*

Sometimes I forget that you are
the God of the darkness as
much as God of the light. Help
me not to light my own fires in the
midst of the dark times, but to press in
further, to allow the uncertainty to push
me deeper into trust.

*"Today is a very serious
day with very serious
consequences."*

But then again, what day,
or person, or relationship,
or moment . . . is not?

9 AUGUST

"In some sense every parent does love their children," she responded, ignoring his second question. "But some parents are too broken to love them well and others are barely able to love them at all."

Like most of us, I left childhood with exit wounds. What I did with those has shaped much of my life. I know I must forgive and honor the good given, or I will doom myself to be stuck in resentments and regrets.

"Among the mysteries of a broken humanity, that too is rather remarkable; to learn, to allow change."

I believe that real and actual change in a human heart and soul makes raising someone from the dead look like child's play. I suppose that both are a form of raising the dead, but the former is so much more miraculous and profound. Only you can do this impossible.

"So then, Mackenzie, may I ask which of your children do you love the most?"

Mack smiled inside. As the kids had come along, he had wrestled to an answer to this very question. "I don't love any one of them more than any of the others. I love each of them differently," *he said, choosing his words carefully. . . . "When I think of each of my children individually, I find that I am especially fond of each one."*

Thank you for looking at me this way— not as a lost number, but as a fragile, unique, magnificent being whom you participated with my parents in creating.

"But what about when they do not behave, or they make choices other than those you would want them to make . . . ? How does that affect your love for them?"

"It doesn't, really. . . . I admit that it does affect me and sometimes I get embarrassed or angry, but even when they act badly, they are still my son or my daughter . . . and they will be forever. What they do might affect my pride, but not my love for them."

Why is it so difficult for us to believe that our love for our own children is but a reflection of the way you love?

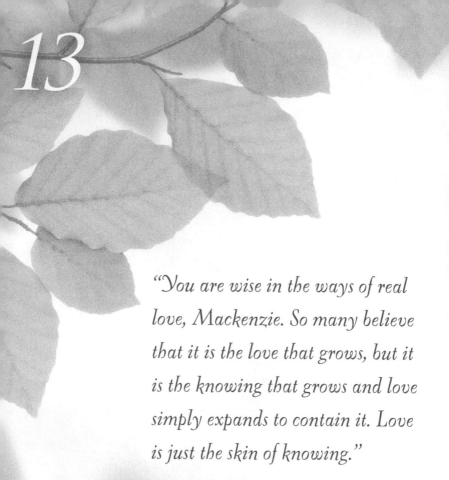

13

> *"You are wise in the ways of real love, Mackenzie. So many believe that it is the love that grows, but it is the knowing that grows and love simply expands to contain it. Love is just the skin of knowing."*

I am susceptible to infatuation; loving myself through someone, something, or an imagination, which is no love at all, since "knowing" destroys such illusions. I want to be known and truly loved, to know and to love. You know me. You love me.

"This is a time for honesty, for truth. You don't believe that Father loves his children very well, do you? You don't truly believe that God is good, do you?"

When darkness is all around, the last thing I risk believing is that you are good and that you are "for" me. I believe the lie that it is safer alone in the dark than with you.

He had no defense. He was lost and he knew it. . . .
"I'm quite a mess, aren't I?"

"Yes, you are." Mack looked up and she smiled back.
"You are a glorious, destructive mess, Mackenzie."

Your divine verdict upon me is that I am a wreck, loved forever, but a wreck, and that there is hope for me, because you specialize in redeeming wrecks.

"I don't have any ability to judge."

"Oh, that is not true. You have already proven yourself very capable, even in our short time together. And besides, you have judged many throughout your life. You have judged the actions and even the motivations of others, as if you somehow knew what those were in truth. . . . you are quite well-practiced in the activity."

While we are at it, I admit that I am a skilled jury and executioner, too—not one of the things I like about how I function, but I don't know how else to survive. Help!

Mack looked up and tried to meet her gaze, but found that when he looked directly at her, his thinking wavered. To peer into her eyes and keep a train of coherent and logical thought seemed to be impossible. He had to look away and into the darkness of the corner of the room hoping to collect himself.

To look true love in the eyes is to face the demand of utter honesty, and thus to stand on the razor's edge of trusting it or going back to my games.

"Judging requires that you think yourself superior over the one you judge. Well, today you will be given the opportunity to put all your ability to use."

The irony is so deep. In one moment, I live with a low view of myself, unlovable, unworthy, etc., and in the next, I am judging those around me. Why don't I know how to love myself without thinking someone else holds a lower card?

19 AUGUST

"And just what will I be judging?"

"Not what. Who."

I know it is never your intent that I am embarrassed or ashamed, but I am. I trust that somehow beginning to understand the appalling way I judge others and myself without light will become part of my liberation.

Mack knew he was thoroughly guilty for being self-centered. How dare he judge anyone else?

You know that my self-centeredness is sometimes because I think too highly of myself, sometimes because I think nothing of myself, and sometimes because I think I am all I have. Yes, I think this qualifies as a "mess."

21

"Why not? Surely there are many people in your world you think deserve judgment. There must be at least a few who are to blame for so much of the pain and suffering."

I do . . . and I am probably one of them. All the big and little ways we cause harm and then justify ourselves. I am so blind to my own darkness and so aware of everyone else's failures. Would you call that hypocrisy? Yeah, that's what I was thinking.

"How far do we go back, Mackenzie? This legacy of brokenness goes all the way back to Adam, what about him? But why stop there? What about God? God started this whole thing. Is God to blame?"

Knowing all that I know now about our ability to damage ourselves and one another, would I choose that you would never have created, that my son or daughter, my friend or enemy, would never have existed? No. So my hope is in you, that you continue to find a way to redeem our brokenness with your presence, grace, and forgiveness.

23 AUGUST

"Isn't that where you are stuck, Mackenzie? Isn't that what fuels The Great Sadness? That God cannot be trusted? Surely, a father like you can judge the Father! . . . Isn't that your just complaint, Mackenzie? That God has failed you. That he failed Missy?"

If you cannot be trusted, that you sometimes are the author of evil, then I am without hope, a planet unhinged from its sun, spinning alone within the icy vastness of a meaningless universe. But I have noticed that even when I believe this lie with my mind, my heart will not allow me to live that way.

"Yes! God is to blame!" The accusation hung in the room as the gavel fell in his heart.

"Then," she said with finality, "if you are able to judge God so easily, then you certainly can judge the world." Again she spoke without emotion. "You must choose two of your children to spend eternity in God's new heavens and new earth, but only two. And you must choose three of your children to spend eternity in hell."

Forgive me for thinking that this was just a game or cosmic experiment to you.

"I'm only asking you to do something that you believe God does. He knows every person ever conceived, and he knows them so much deeper and clearer than you will ever know your own children. He loves each one according to his knowledge of the being of that son or daughter. You believe he will condemn most to an eternity of torment, away from His presence and apart from His love. Is that not true?"

I remember wanting to believe that. I used to think I was better than other people.

"I suppose I do. I've just never thought about it like this. I just assumed somehow God could do that. Talking about hell was always sort of an abstract conversation, not about anyone I truly . . . " Mack hesitated, realizing what he was about to say would sound ugly, "not about anyone that I truly cared about."

I am deeply grateful knowing that Jesus is not an abstract ideology or doctrine but your living, breathing word who cared enough to become the conversation!

"So you suppose, then, that God does this easily, but you cannot? Come now, Mackenzie. Which three of your five children will you sentence to hell? . . . You are the judge, and you must choose."

"I don't want to be the judge."

I suspect that is part of my training; looking at the world from the neck up, calculated, rational, intellectual. Please connect my head to my heart so I can be a whole person. I don't want to be the judge.

"I can't. I can't. I won't!"

The woman just stood watching and waiting. Finally he looked at her, pleading with his eyes. "Could I go instead? I'll go in their place. Would that work? Could I do that? Please, let me go for my children, please, I would be happy to . . . Please, I'm begging you."

This love, where I would take my child's pain if I could, would even willingly die in their stead, that depth of loving must be sourced in the way you love.

"*Mackenzie, Mackenzie,*" *she whispered.*
"*Now you sound like Jesus. You have*
judged well. I am so proud of you."

When we love with your love, this self-giving, other-centered love, we would gladly damn ourselves that one of our brothers or sisters will no longer hurt. That is the mystery of your love that I want to be the constant of my life.

"But I haven't judged anything."

"Oh, but you have. You have judged them worthy of love, even if it cost you everything. That is how Jesus loves."

That's it! The only judge I ever want to be is one who judges others, this creation, and even myself worthy of love, regardless of the cost. Father, Jesus, and Holy Spirit, please be that loving in me.

"And now you know Papa's heart," she added, "who loves all his children perfectly."

The nearest I come to plummeting the depth of your loving is this mysterious willing-to-die-for-them love I have for my children. And then I hear you whisper, "How much more the Father . . ."

"I love Papa, whoever she is. She's amazing, but she's not anything like the God I've known."

"Maybe your understanding of God is wrong."

It is both horrifying and liberating to find out that we were utterly wrong about you. Athanasius said, "The God of all is good, and supremely noble by nature. Therefore, he is the lover of the human race."

2

"Did God use her to punish me for what I did to my father? That isn't fair. She didn't deserve this. I might have, but they didn't."

"Is that who your God is? It is no wonder you are drowning in your sorrow. Papa isn't like that, Mackenzie. . . . This was not his doing."

I thought you sometimes were the author of evil for "good" purposes. That is one of the lies I believed that kept me from trusting you. I was wrong . . . again.

"[Papa] doesn't stop a lot of things that cause him pain. Your world is severely broken. You demanded your independence, and now you are angry with the one who loved you enough to give it to you. Nothing is as it should be, as Papa desires it to be, as it will be one day. Right now your world is lost in darkness and chaos, and horrible things happen to those that he is especially fond of."

You are a wonder! You even respect our darkened wishes and love us toward the light without coercion.

"Then why doesn't he do something about it?"

"He already has . . ."

"You mean what Jesus did?"

"Haven't you seen the wounds on Papa too? . . .
He chose the way of the cross where mercy
triumphs over justice because of love."

he cross—the most
awful and majestic
mystery of the cosmos.
Other-centered, self-giving
love! I don't understand.

5

"But I still don't understand why Missy had to die."

"She didn't have to, Mackenzie. This was no plan of Papa's. Papa has never needed evil to accomplish his good purposes. It is you humans who have embraced evil and Papa has responded with goodness. What happened to Missy was the work of evil and no one in your world is immune from it."

Thank you for never forcing us into love, into healing, into freedom. Sometimes I want you to "fix" me, but I know in my heart that true love wouldn't act that way.

"Return from your independence. Give up being his judge and know Papa for who he is. Then you will be able to embrace his love in the midst of your pain, instead of pushing him away with your self-centered perception of how you think the universe should be. Papa has crawled inside of your world to be with you, to be with Missy."

Lord God, I give up. Teach me who you are.

7 SEPTEMBER

"I don't want to be a judge any more.
I really do want to trust Papa."

"Now that sounds like the start of the
trip home."

And those of us with orphaned hearts,
We watch from outside in.
The call of "home" is ever faint,
But we're drawn to it again
and again
and again.

8

"This life is only the anteroom of a greater reality to come. No one reaches their potential in your world. It's only preparation for what Papa had in mind all along."

I am no longer dazzled by my own opinions. I am scared speechless that someone may have listened. I am pitiful and yet with an eternal destiny. Did you really know what you were doing when you included me? (Insecure Prayer #94)

"Mackenzie, judgment is not about destruction, but about setting things right."

Punishment has never set anything right. I used to think that you were a punitive god who was out to make people pay. Then Jesus came along, and I found out you were out to pay for the mess that people made.

His constant companion, The Great Sadness, was gone. It was as if it had been washed away in the mists of the waterfall as he emerged from behind its curtain. Its absence felt odd, perhaps even uncomfortable. For the past years it had defined for him what was normal, but now unexpectedly it had vanished. Normal is a myth, he thought to himself.

I have defined normal as if my pain would be ever present, eternal. Pain gave me a point of reference, and as strange as it sounds, I am afraid of losing it.

The Great Sadness would not be part of his identity any longer. He knew now that Missy wouldn't care if he refused to put it on. In fact, she wouldn't want him to huddle in that shroud and would likely grieve for him if he did. He wondered who he would be now that he was letting all that go—to walk into each day without the guilt and despair that had sucked the colors of life out of every thing.

What do I do now? Who am I apart from this pain I have held close for so long?

"I love Sarayu," Mack exclaimed as he stood,
somewhat surprised at his own transparency.

"Me too!" Jesus stated with emphasis.

I forget that within your Oneness,
you love one another in particular. I
forget that my ability to love like this
originates in you. Please help me remember.

13

"Actually, with her everything is normal and elegantly simple. Because you are so lost and independent you bring to her many complications, and as a result you find even her simplicity profound."

I realize the more complicated I am the further from being a child I have become. Children run to you without concern while we adults stand in the shadows and wait an invitation. Somewhere we believed the lie that we were no longer children.

"But as for, 'Is any of this real?' Far more real that you can imagine." Jesus paused for a moment to get Mack's full attention. "A better question might be, 'What is real?'"

I have allowed my five senses to define the "real," but how do I put love in a test tube, or delight, joy, grace and kindness, laughter and friendship, dignity and destiny? Please teach me to relax and let the invisibles be fully "real" and fully mystery.

Gently he spoke, "Mack, she was never alone. I never left her; we never left her not for one instant. I could no more abandon her, or you, than I could abandon myself. . . . She may have been only six years old, but Missy and I are friends. We talk."

Y ou never left when I raised my fist to your face or when I cursed. When I ran, you stayed closer than my breath and waited. If you would not abandon me in all my rebellion, why am I tempted to believe you would abandon me in my need?

16

The tears flowed freely now, but even Mack noticed this time it was different. He was no longer alone.

Thank you!

Although he was a little surprised when his first step found the lake bottom up to his ankles. The next one took him up to midcalf, and the next up to just below his knees. He looked back to see Jesus standing on the shore, watching him. He wasn't sure why it wasn't working this time, but he was determined to press on.

"This always works better when we do it together, don't you think?" Jesus asked smiling.

Oh yeah, you don't heal me so I can now be independent. You heal me for participation.

"*Still more to learn I guess.*" *It didn't matter to him, he realized, whether he had to swim the distance or walk on water, as wonderful as the latter was. What mattered was that Jesus was with him. Perhaps he was beginning to trust him after all, even if it were only baby steps.*

I don't fear the spotlight when I know the one shining on me is especially fond of me.

"*Thank you for being with me, for talking to me about Missy. It just felt so huge and terrifying. It doesn't hold the same power now.*"

"*The darkness hides the true size of fears and lies and regrets,*" Jesus explained. "*The truth is they are more shadow than reality, so they seem bigger in the dark. When the light shines into the places they live inside you, you start to see them for what they are.*"

I know my silence enhances darkness where lies and fears grow larger. I want to be an in-the-light person.

"So what do I do now?"

"What you're already doing,
Mack, learning to live loved."

Could I dare believe it is this simple, learning to live loved, without any agenda? I will be still now and listen for your answer.

21

"What we desire is for you to 're-turn' to us, and then we come and make our home inside you, and then we share. The friendship is real, not merely imagined. We're meant to experience this life, your life, together, in a dialogue, sharing the journey."

Jesus, you have crossed all worlds and found us. Now you invite us to walk with you in honest relationship and promised that as we do, the very life you share with your Father and Spirit will come to ever-increasing expression in and through us.

Mack watched, amazed, as Jesus started to dodge this way and that, trying to keep up with the fish, and finally gave up. He looked at Mack, excited as a little kid. "Isn't he great? I'll probably never catch him."

"Why don't you just command him to . . . bite your hook?"

"What would be the fun in that?"

Sometimes it is difficult to believe that the Lord of all has become fully human and that "fun" would matter to you like it does to me.

Mack didn't know whether to laugh or cry.
He realized how much he had come to love
this man, this man who was also God.

There has always been something about you, Jesus, that has always drawn me in your direction, and dare I admit it even to myself, to truly love you? I love you! I do! I love you!

"Have you ever noticed that in your pain you assume the worst of me? I've been talking to you for a long time, but today was the first time you could hear it, and all those other times weren't a waste either. Like little cracks in the wall, one at a time, but woven together they prepared you for today. You have to take the time to prepare the soil if you want to embrace the seed."

Thank you for not evaluating me from the infinite distance of a disapproving heart but for dwelling in my process.

"I'm not sure why we resist you so much? It seems kind of stupid now."

"It's all part of the timing of grace. Each choice ripples throughout time and relationships, bouncing off of other choices. And out of what seems to be a huge mess, Papa weaves a magnificent tapestry. Only Papa can work all this out, and she does it with grace."

I bow today to your wisdom and generosity of heart, to your kind grace and intention. You are the Grand Weaver. Please take my colors and add them to yours and make something magnificent.

"So I guess all I can do is follow her,"
Mack concluded.

"Yep, that's the point. Now you're
beginning to understand what it
means to be truly human."

A re you telling me that you didn't have a wonderful plan for my life all mapped out that I have totally bungled and mismanaged? You didn't expect me to "be farther down the road" than I am, and that you are not mad at me or disappointed? (Insecure Prayer #131)

27 SEPTEMBER

"Well Mack, our final destiny is not the picture of Heaven that you have stuck in your head—you know, the image of pearly gates and streets of gold. Instead it's a new cleansing of this universe, so it will indeed look a lot like here."

Part of my fear of death is that I would have to exit this profound home I love, with its savory splendor and enter an antiseptic and sterile place marked by boredom and costume jewelry. That this universe is part of my destiny gives me hope.

28

"It is a picture of my bride, the Church: individuals who together form a spiritual city with a living river flowing through the middle, and on both shores trees growing with fruit that will heal the hurt and sorrows of the nations. And this city is always open, and each gate into it is made of a single pearl . . ."

I want to be part of a living Church from whom flows a river of living water and who exists for the healing of the hurts and sorrows of the nations. We are deeply wounded and filled with sadness.

"That would be me!" Jesus saw Mack's question and explained, "Pearls, Mack. The only precious stone made by pain, suffering and—finally—death."

Jesus, you are our always-open gate. Thank you for bearing our wrath, our scorn, our brutality, and emerging as a precious stone upon which we build our lives.

"I get it. You are the way in, but—
You're talking about the church as
this woman you're in love with; I'm
pretty sure I haven't met her. She's
not the place I go to on Sunday."

Many of us are cynical and sad. We mistook the religious system and enterprise for the real thing, but instead of looking for her, we found it easier to be mad at her impersonator. Heal our eyes so that we can find her whether hidden inside a system or running free.

"It's simple, Mack. It's all about relationships and simply sharing life. What we are doing right now—just doing this—and being open and available to others around us. My church is all about people and life is all about relationships. You can't build it. It's my job and I'm actually pretty good at it."

I know vulnerability and authenticity breed the same, and both are essential for community. I see this in you. May others see it in me.

For Mack these words were like a breath of fresh air! Simple. Not a bunch of exhausting work and long list of demands, and not the sitting in endless meetings staring at the backs of people's heads, people he really didn't even know. Just sharing life.

George MacDonald said, "What child . . . would prefer a sermon to a glorious kite . . . with God for a playmate, in the blue wind tossing it in the golden void! One might part with the kite and wind and sun, and go down to the grave for brothers—but surely not that they might be admitted to an everlasting prayer meeting."

3 OCTOBER

This seemed too simple! Again he caught himself.
Perhaps it was because humans are so utterly
lost and independent that we take what is
simple and make it complex. So he thought twice
about messing with what he was beginning to
understand. To begin asking his jumbled mess of
questions at this moment felt like throwing a dirt
clod into a little pool of clear water.

Help me rest in this moment of simple understanding and not race to find something else. For now, let this be enough.

"Mack, you don't need to have it all figured out. Just be with me."

I have always needed to figure everything out. To simply "be" with you, to let go of control and trust the relationship that is at the center of everything, fills me with a disturbing hope.

5

*"As well-intentioned as it might be, you know
that religious machinery can chew up people!"
Jesus said with a bite of his own. "An awful
lot of what is done in my name has nothing to
do with me and is often, even if unintentional,
very contrary to my purposes."*

And yet you love the religious person . . .
you love me. Those religious people who
do so much damage are my people.
In you, there is hope for us all.

"I don't create institutions—never have, never will," Jesus said. . . . "Marriage is not an institution. It's a relationship."

What a gift! If we allow it, there is nothing quite like marriage to expose and annihilate our self-centeredness and to raise to the surface some of what is the most precious gold hidden in our souls.

"People are afraid of uncertainty, afraid of the future. These institutions, these structures and ideologies, are all a vain effort to create some sense of certainty and security where there isn't any. It's all false! Systems cannot provide you security, only I can."

It seems we will trust "the works of our own hands," the systems and institutions we created, rather than you. Maybe we think our own works are easier to control. Then we find out that control is a myth and what we created owns us. Thank you for not leaving us to our own unfriendly devices!

"I don't have an agenda here, Mack. Just the opposite," Jesus interjected. "I came to give you Life to the fullest. My life." Mack was still straining to understand. "The simplicity and purity of enjoying a growing friendship?"

I have spent my life trying to manufacture peace, hope, and joy and then pretended to be successful. Jesus, you live loved with no agenda. You reach into your own soul, drawing out your inner world, and put it in us all. Thank you for wanting us to know what you do and for sharing such a life.

"If you try to live this without me, without the ongoing dialogue of us sharing this journey together, it will be like trying to walk on the water by yourself. You can't. And when you try, however well-intentioned, you're going to sink."

Thank you for respecting me enough to let me try this on my own. Thank you, too, for letting me sink, for allowing me to reach the end of my own resources, to look up and away from myself. And thank you for waiting for my foolishness to fail.

10

*"Have you ever tried to save someone who
was drowning? . . . It's extremely hard
to rescue someone unless they are willing
to trust you. . . . That's all I ask of you.
When you start to sink, let me rescue you."*

I finally admit, I am sinking! I've done my
part. Please do your part and rescue me!
What? You're not going to rescue me
on my terms? Are you saying you want me to
"actually" trust you, not just say that I do?

11 OCTOBER

It seemed like a simple request, but Mack was used to being the lifeguard, not the one drowning. "Jesus, I'm not sure I know how to . . ."

"Let me show you. Just keep giving me the little bit you have, and together we'll watch it grow."

Today, I am not even sure where that little bit is, so please search my soul and find it and know that is what I am giving to you. I want the little to grow.

"Sitting here with you, in this moment, it doesn't seem that hard. But when I think about my regular life back home, I don't know how to keep it as simple as you're suggesting. I'm stuck in that same grasp for control everyone else is."

I suppose I am going to learn to trust that grace will also be there for me in the normal and mundane and the everyday. Your character is my guarantee.

13

"I don't know how to change it all."

"No one is asking you to!" Jesus said tenderly. "That is Sarayu's task and she knows how to do it without brutalizing anyone. This whole thing is a process, not an event."

You know I am not a big fan of process. I would rather take a blue or red pill or have an extreme soul makeover. But I also know that true and lasting change takes time, and I hear you whisper that I am worth your time.

"All I want from you is to trust me with what little you can, and grow in loving people around you with the same love I share with you. It's not your job to change them, or convince them. You are free to love without an agenda."

I confess that I try to change people because I believe I am better at it than you. I don't want to wait that long. I also admit my track record isn't that good. It's frustrating. People are so uncooperative. You understand? You talkin' to me?

"Institutions, systems, ideologies, and all the vain, futile efforts of humanity that go with them are everywhere, and interaction with all of it is unavoidable. But I can give you freedom to overcome any system of power in which you find yourself, be it religious, economic, social, or political. You will grow in the freedom to be inside or outside all kinds of systems and to move freely between and among them. Together, you and I can be in it and not of it."

When all is said and done, I do . . . want to be free!

"But so many of the people I care about seem to be both in it and of it!"

"Mack, I love them. And you wrongly judge many of them. For those who are both in it and of it, we must find ways to love and serve them, don't you think? Remember, the people who know me are the ones who are free to live and love without any agenda."

Jesus, you once told me that your Father judges no one (John 5:22). Free me to be like that, please?

"Does that mean," asked Mack, *"that all roads will lead to you?"*

"Not at all," smiled Jesus. *"Most roads don't lead anywhere. What it does mean is that I will travel any road to find you."*

And you have! It's never been the road I chose that mattered to you; it has been that I was on it. You even left the ninety-nine, just to find the one . . . just to find me.

Papa was reclining on an old Adirondack chair, eyes closed, soaking in the sun.

"What's this? God has time to catch a few rays? Don't you have anything better to do this afternoon?"

"Mack, you have no idea what I'm doing right now."

I thrill that you are beyond my ability to comprehend, that you are good beyond my understanding, that you never do anything for just one reason, but your purposes are multiple and grace-filled, that you are uncontrollable and an interferer. I bend my knee. I am in awe!

"I have been pretty hard on you. . . . I had no idea I had presumed to be your judge. It sounds so horribly arrogant. . . . I am so sorry. I really had no idea . . ." Mack shook his head sadly.

"But that is in the past now, where it belongs. I don't even want your sorrow for it, Mack. I just want us to grow on together without it."

Papa, deliver me from judging— but not all at once, for I am not sure how much of me would be left.

"She loved that story [the legend of the Multnomah Princess] so much."

"Of course she did. That's how she came to appreciate what Jesus did for her and the whole human race. Stories about a person willing to exchange their life for another are a golden thread in your world, revealing both your need and my heart."

May my eyes be open to seeing you everywhere, even in our fables and mythologies, in our poetry and fairy tales, in our lyrics and imagery—this golden thread of your presence and story.

"Just because I work incredible good out of unspeakable tragedies doesn't mean I orchestrate the tragedies. Don't ever assume that my using something means I caused it or that I need it to accomplish my purposes. That will only lead you to false notions about me. Grace doesn't depend on suffering to exist, but where there is suffering you will find grace in many facets and colors."

Forgive me for ever thinking that the end justifies the means, that the many are worth more than the one, that you are a wolf in sheep's clothing.

"I have totally misunderstood who you are in my life."

"Not totally, Mack. We've had some wonderful moments, too. So let's not make more of it than it is."

Whenever I have admitted my misunderstanding of your life and character, I have heard you speak to me.

"But I always liked Jesus better than you. He seemed so gracious and you seemed so . . ."

"Mean? Sad, isn't it? He came to show people who I am and most folks only believe it about him. They still play us off like good cop/bad cop most of the time, especially the religious folk. When they want people to do what they think is right, they need a stern God. When they need forgiveness, they run to Jesus."

Forgive me, Jesus, for believing and then telling lies about your Father.

"But why me? I mean, why Mackenzie Allen Phillips? Why do you love someone who is such a screw-up? After all the things I've felt in my heart toward you and all the accusations I made, why would you even bother to keep trying to get through to me?"

"Because that is what love does," answered Papa.

I am beginning to understand that you, Jesus, Papa, Holy Spirit, have loved one another from all eternity, and I am beginning to believe that you relate to each of us out of your way of being together. That changes everything.

"I don't wonder what you will do or what choices you will make. I already know. . . . when you don't hear me the first time, I'm not frustrated or disappointed, I'm thrilled. Only forty-six more times to go."

I so easily forget that you know me completely, that I never surprise you or slip something by you. I forget that you relate to me within your knowing of me, and that is a comfort and a hope.

"It's not about feeling guilty. Guilt'll never help you find freedom in me. The best it can do is make you try harder to conform to some ethic on the outside. I'm about the inside."

I am all about feeling guilt and regret. I exist with a tangible sense of being a failure, a disappointment. I am so susceptible to someone else shaming me into allegiance and performance. I need to stop, but I don't know how. I don't want to live like this. Heal me so I am able to live from the inside out.

"Hiding inside lies—I guess I've done that one way or another most of my life."

"Honey, you're a survivor. No shame in that. Your daddy hurt you something fierce. Life hurt you. Lies are one of the easiest places for survivors to run. It gives you a sense of safety, in a place where you only have to depend on yourself. But it's a dark place, isn't it?"

It's true! I am a survivor, a hider, a liar. I scramble and shade the truth. My "yes" is not quite "yes," and my "no" is rarely a simple "no." Help!

"Take the risks of honesty. When you mess up again, ask for forgiveness again. It's a process, honey, and life is real enough without having to be obscured by lies. And remember, I am bigger than your lies. I can work beyond them. But that doesn't make them right and doesn't stop the damage they do or the hurt they cause others."

Could I just apologize? Apologizing lets me keep power and control, and it's a lot easier than asking for forgiveness.

29

"Faith does not grow in the house of certainty."

Papa, I don't want to be an old person one day who looks back on their life and asks, "What would it have been like to take the risks involved in faith, in letting go of control and certainty? What would it have been like to actually trust?" I don't want to be that person.

"My life inside you will appropriate risk and uncertainty to transform you by your own choices into a truth teller, and that will be a miracle greater than raising the dead."

To be open, authentic, honest, transparent, simply a truth teller— that would be a dream come true. I want you to know that I am open to the miraculous . . . and that is the truth.

"Will you please forgive me?" Mack finally offered.

"Did that a long time ago, Mack. If you don't believe me, ask Jesus. He was there."

You, the innocent, died for the guilty. That is a strange justice. It cost you dearly to find a way into my profound darkness and call me into the light. Even when I refuse, I am still met, received, and embraced, but I know as long as I am tethered to the darkness, I will not know the healing joy of the process of forgiveness completed.

"*People are tenacious when it comes to the treasure of their imaginary independence. . . . They find their identity and worth in their brokenness and guard it with every ounce of strength they have. No wonder grace has such little attraction. In that sense you have tried to lock the door of your heart from the inside.*"

I have always said I wanted to be whole and then resisted the invitation to go through what it took to be whole. It seemed easier to believe that I didn't matter, but you keep telling me otherwise.

"But I didn't succeed."

"That's because my love is a lot bigger than your stupidity," Papa said with a wink. "I used your choices to work perfectly into my purposes."

I fell for the myth that I could manipulate you with religious words and magic, that I was somehow more powerful and cunning than you, that I could find a way to make you stop loving me.

"True love never forces."

Thank you!

"If it were only that simple, Mackenzie. Nobody knows what horror I have saved the world from 'cuz people can't see what never happened."

I am skilled at blaming you for everything that "goes wrong." Because I thought you were sometimes the author of evil, I stopped thanking you for a daughter's smile, or the taste of a red grapefruit, or the glimpse of the ocean swell, or the sound of friendly laughter, or . . .

I was wrong. So today, thank you for . . .

5

"All evil flows from independence, and independence is your choice. If I were to simply revoke all the choices of independence, the world as you know it would cease to exist and love would have no meaning."

Independence has never been a part of your character, so it truly is my choice, my declaration, and my devastation. Thank you for including me into your dance of submitted affection, which seems foreign and yet is so native to my design.

"This world is not a playground where I keep all my children free from evil. Evil is the chaos of this age that you brought to me, but it will not have the final say."

How incredible and "other" is your character that you would be at work tirelessly redeeming our disasters, even while we blame you for them all.

"If I take away the consequences of people's choices, I destroy the possibility of love. Love that is forced is no love at all."

Genuine love requires genuine freedom and real risk. Jesus, thank you for picking up the tab for what we have done and are doing in our freedom. Thank you, too, for allowing us to experience with you the consequences of our choices. It's a part of growing up.

"You and this Creation are incredible, whether you understand that or not. You are wonderful beyond imagination."

We are so terribly hard on ourselves, our own worst critics. Give us glimpses through your eyes that we might catch sight of the wonderful we are that is beyond imagination.

"Don't forget that in the midst of all your pain and heartache, you are surrounded by beauty, the wonder of Creation, art, your music, and culture, the sounds of laughter and love, of whispered hopes and celebrations, of new life and transformation, of reconciliation and forgiveness."

Sometimes the dark drowns out the remembering of all the joys you have given me, the people in and through whom you have added delight and wonder to my life. Today, I thank you for some of these precious gifts . . .

"*So whose choices should we countermand, Mackenzie? Perhaps I should never have created? Perhaps Adam should have been stopped before he chose independence? What about your choice to have another daughter, or your father's choice to beat his son? You demand your independence, but then complain that I actually love you enough to give it to you.*"

I'm such a whiner and complainer. My accusations expose my lack of trust in your character. It helps that, unlike me, you are not weak and insecure about who you are. Your affection keeps spanning the gap created by my grumbling. Thank you!

11 NOVEMBER

"My purposes are not for my comfort, or yours. My purposes are always and only an expression of love. I purpose to work life out of death, to bring freedom out of brokenness and turn darkness to light."

I believe, Jesus, that there is no darkness in you or Father, and certainly not in the Holy Spirit, not even a hint, ever. You are a family of only light, love, and oneness, who has responded to my darkness, brokenness, and death by removing, healing, and resurrecting.

*"What you see as chaos, I see as a fractal.
All things must unfold, even though it puts all
those I love in the midst of a world of horrible
tragedies—even the one closest to me."*

In the midst of this chaos we call life, open my eyes to look first for the Spirit's presence and redeeming genius.

13

"Yup, I love that boy." Papa looked away and shook her head. "Everything's about him, you know. One day you folk will understand what he gave up. There are just no words."

Papa, I grew up being taught that Jesus had to bear your wrath only to find out it was our rage he submitted himself to in order to meet and embrace us as we are, and that you three worked it into your purposes before creation (Hebrews 12:3).

"Like I said, everything is about him. Creation and history are all about Jesus. He is the very center of our purpose and in him we are now fully human, so our purpose and your destiny are forever linked. You might say we have put all our eggs in the one human basket. There is no Plan B."

Jesus, you are the only hope for me as a human being, for us as humanity, and for the created cosmos. I cannot comprehend the nature of a love so willing.

"Papa, can you help me understand something? What exactly did Jesus accomplish by dying?"

She was still looking out into the forest. "Oh," she waved her hand. "Nothing much. Just the substance of everything that love purposed from before the foundations of Creation," Papa stated matter of factly.

From forever you have had each of us in mind and have never been distracted from that affection.

16

Papa sat forward and crossed her arms on the table. "Honey, you asked me what Jesus accomplished on the cross; so now listen to me carefully: through his death and resurrection, I am now fully reconciled to the world."

"The whole world? You mean those who believe in you, right?"

"The whole world, Mack."

Your words, not mine (2 Corinthians 5:18–19). I am humbled and undone!

"All I am telling you is that reconciliation is a two way street, and I have done my part, totally, completely, finally. It is not the nature of love to force a relationship but it is the nature of love to open the way."

What keeps me from you? Why do I resist such love? Why do I run from the one who knows me best and loves me most?

"Have you been with me the entire time?" inquired Mack.

"Of course. I am always with you."

"Then how come I didn't know it?" asked Mack.

"For you to know or not," she explained, "has nothing at all to do with whether I am actually here or not. I am always with you; sometimes I want you to be aware in a special way—more intentional."

I once thought I had to feel you to believe. When I do sense you, I am grateful, but it isn't essential anymore. I am growing to know you. Today, I rest in that.

"Will I always be able to see you or hear you like I do now, even if I am back home?"

"Mackenzie, you can always talk to me and I will always be with you, whether you sense my presence or not."

"I know that now, but how will I hear you?"

"You will learn to hear my thoughts in yours, Mackenzie," she reassured him.

You do know how deaf I am? I have lived confused by many voices. Teach me to discern your voice, to hear your thoughts in mine, to hear you right where life happens.

"What if I make mistakes?"

Sarayu laughed, the sound like tumbling water, only set to music. "Of course you will make mistakes; everybody makes mistakes, but you will begin to better recognize my voice as we continue to grow our relationship."

Teach me to laugh at myself.

21

"I don't want to make mistakes," Mack grunted.

"Oh, Mackenzie," responded Sarayu, "mistakes are a part of life, and Papa works his purpose in them, too."

I am thinking this is a sign of growth for me; I am at a place where I think a mistake is at least a possibility. I am so full of myself.

"Emotions are the colors of the soul. When you don't feel, the world becomes dull and colorless. Just think how The Great Sadness reduced the range of color in your life down to monotones and flat grays."

Please heal me so that I not only experience the range of emotions, but I can actually begin to trust them. Thank you for emotions!

"Mackenzie!" she chided, her words flowing with affection. "The Bible doesn't teach you to follow rules. It is a picture of Jesus. While words may tell you what God is like and even what he may want from you, you cannot do any of it on your own."

The day is coming when we won't need a single rule. We will be horrified at even the thought of not loving our brothers and sisters more than ourselves, and we will consider it an honor beyond words to give our lives for their betterment. There is no barbed wire in God's kingdom.

"Life and living is in him and in no other."

Jesus, you are the source and meaning of my existence. Without you, I will never know myself, let alone anyone else.

"*It is true that relationships are a whole lot messier than rules, but rules will never give you answers to the deep questions of the heart and they will never love you.*"

I know my relationships are messy because of my own damage and the messy I bring to them, but being loved by even a broken person is far superior than snuggling with rules and expectations.

"Religion is about having the right answers, and some of their answers are right. But I am about the process that takes you to the living answer and once you get to him, he will change you from the inside."

It has always been easier to be right than to love.

"So, will I see you again?" he asked hesitantly.

"Of course. You might see me in a piece of art, or music, or silence, or through people, or in Creation, or in your joy and sorrow. My ability to communicate is limitless, living and transforming, and it will always be tuned to Papa's goodness and love."

Holy Spirit, help me take my "church glasses" off and see what is really going on in Jesus' world and open my heart and mind to however you want to sing to me.

"And you will hear and see me in the Bible in fresh ways. Just don't look for rules and principles; look for relationship—a way of coming to be with us."

How can I see in fresh ways, unless I admit that my current seeing is flawed . . . my current seeing is flawed.

"It still won't be the same as having you sit on the bow of my boat."

"No, it will be far better than you've yet known, Mackenzie. And when you finally sleep in this world, we'll have an eternity together—face-to-face."

Holy Spirit, help me see you inside the everyday conversations, sunsets, laughter and sadness of my life. Thank you for giving me a future and a hope. I love you.

As Mack ate, he listened to the banter between the three. They talked and laughed like old friends who knew one another intimately. As he thought about it, that was assuredly more true for his hosts than anyone inside or outside Creation. He was envious of the carefree but respectful conversation and wondered what it would take to share that with Nan and maybe even with some friends.

What it would take to share that?" is the question we face. Most of the time I don't see how I can possibly get from here to there, but Holy Spirit, you are brilliant.

"Why do you love me, when I have nothing to offer you?"

"If you think about it, Mack," Jesus answered, "it should be very freeing to know that you can offer us nothing, at least not anything that can add or take away from who we are. . . . That should alleviate any pressure to perform."

I am not acceptable"—the lie that becomes the mantra of our lives. But we are accepted, warts and all, and when this freedom is born and grows in our broken souls, we begin to inhale affection and exhale grace.

2

"Then why did you give us those commandments?" asked Mack.

"Actually, we wanted you to give up trying to be righteous on your own. It was a mirror to reveal just how filthy your face gets when you live independently."

I looked in the mirror and saw the dirt, grime, and filth of my choices. Religion demanded I use the mirror to clean myself. It never worked, no matter how hard I scraped. Then you whispered the mirror was only meant to point me to you, and you would wash my heart and cleanse my soul.

*"That's why Jesus fulfilled all of it for you—
so that it no longer has jurisdiction over you.
And the Law that once contained impossible
demands—Thou Shall Not . . .—actually
becomes a promise we fulfill in you."*

This means that because of your life
in me, I will become a person who
does not lie, steal, commit adultery,
lust after what another has, create false idols
around which to center my life, etc.

"Those who are afraid of freedom are those who cannot trust us to live in them. Trying to keep the law is actually a declaration of independence, a way of keeping control."

A wet dog smells worse than a skunk, yet both are perfume to the soul when standing next to a person who actually believes he or she is doing it right by the Law.

*"And contrary to what you might think,
I have a great fondness for uncertainty.
Rules cannot bring freedom; they only
have the power to accuse."*

Only when I do not know, when I am uncertain, only then do I stop and ask for directions and listen. How lost am I when I am certain I am not?

"I give you an ability to respond and your response is to be free to love and serve in every situation, and therefore each moment is different and unique and wonderful. Because I am your ability to respond, I have to be present in you. If I simply gave you a responsibility, I would not have to be with you at all. It would now be a task to perform, an obligation to be met, something to fail."

An ability to respond versus responsibility, freedom and relationship versus religion and performance . . . two opposed worlds.

7

"There is expectancy of being together, of laughing and talking. That expectancy has no concrete definition; it is alive and dynamic and everything that emerges from our being together is a unique gift shared by no one else. But what happens if I change that 'expectancy' to an 'expectation'—spoken or unspoken? Suddenly, law has entered into our relationship. Our living friendship rapidly deteriorates into a dead thing with rules and requirements. It is no longer about you and me, but about what friends are supposed to do, or the responsibilities of a good friend."

I don't want that!

"Are you saying you have no expectations of me?"

Papa now spoke up, "Honey, I've never placed an expectation on you or anyone else. The idea behind expectations requires that someone does not know the future or the outcome and is trying to control behavior to get the desired result. Humans try to control behavior largely through expectations. I know you and everything about you. Why would I have an expectation other than what I already know? That would be foolish. And beyond that, because I have no expectations, you never disappoint me."

I LOVE this about you!

"What? You've never been disappointed in me?" Mack was trying hard to digest this.

"Never!" Papa stated emphatically. "What I do have is a constant and living expectancy in our relationship, and I give you an ability to respond to any situation and circumstance in which you find yourself."

Never once, in ten thousand sermons that I have heard, have I suspected that my God has no expectations of me. The whole religious world moves on the threat of divine expectations. What is going to happen when we get the point?

*"To the degree that you resort to
expectations and responsibilities, to that
degree you neither know me nor trust me."*

*"And," interjected Jesus, "to that degree
you will live in fear."*

The thought that Papa is not disappointed in me is
too much to bear. How could it be? God is not
disgusted with my issues and me? Come on. There
has to be a catch. Indeed! You caught me in your love.

"If you put God at the top, what does that really mean and how much is enough? How much time do you give me before you can go on about the rest of your day, the part that interests you so much more?" Papa again interrupted. "You see, Mackenzie, I don't just want a piece of you and a piece of your life. Even if you were able, which you are not, to give me the biggest piece, that is not what I want. I want all of you and all of every part of you and your day."

I want that too.

Jesus now spoke again. "Mack, I don't want to be first among a list of values; I want to be at the center of everything.

*A*nd you are! All that we love, all that we are burdened by, the music of our souls, the longings, the hurts, the joys—all have their origin in you, Jesus, and in your relationship with Father and Holy Spirit. Teach me to stop trying to relate to you as a priority.

13 DECEMBER

"Rather than a pyramid, I want to be the center of a mobile, where everything in your life—your friends, family, occupation, thoughts, activities—is connected to me but moves with the wind, in and out and back and forth, in an incredible dance of being."

"Nothing is a ritual, Mack," said Papa.

I am grateful for traditions, celebrations, for the sense of ritual that centers my thoughts and even my heart, but if I miss what and who these are pointing to, they become deadly poison.

"Daddy, I'm so sorry! Daddy, I love you!" The light of his words seemed to blast darkness out of his father's colors, turning them blood red. They exchanged sobbing words of confession and forgiveness, as a love greater than either one healed them.

It is liberation to realize what my dad endured in his history and how great he did with what he was handed. We all need forgiving. We all need to forgive.

15

Mack shook his head, "You're still messing with me, aren't you?"

"Always," he said with a warm smile, and then answered Mack's next question before it was asked. "This morning you're going to need a father. C'mon now and let's get going."

Mack nodded. He didn't bother to ask where they might be heading out to. If Papa had wanted him to know, he would have told him.

Trust! It seems so slow to appear, but then I catch a glimpse of it, and it makes me grin.

"We are coming full circle. Forgiving your dad yesterday was a significant part of your being able to know me as Father today. . . . Today we are on a healing trail to bring closure to this part of your journey—not just for you, but for others as well."

Wounds, terror, and trauma cut their mark in the soul. Never a man hurt his child who was not terribly hurt himself. That is no excuse! But it does open the door of compassion.

"At this point all I have to offer you as an answer is my love and goodness, and my relationship with you. I did not purpose Missy's death, but that doesn't mean I can't use it for good."

Sometimes I think I want an answer, but what I really want is to know you understand, that you are close enough to wipe away my tears, to feel your tenderness, to sense you are here with me. Thank you for knowing when words are not going to heal my heart, but presence will.

"I do trust you . . ." And suddenly, it was like a new thought, surprising and wonderful. "Papa, I do trust you!"

I do want to trust you! You know that I do. And you also know I am afraid of what that means.

"This is not about shaming you. I don't do humiliation, or guilt, or condemnation. They don't produce one speck of wholeness or righteousness, and that is why they were nailed into Jesus on the cross."

I know that shame has destroyed my ability to distinguish between an observation and a value statement. I fight desperately to hide the obvious and overreact when someone, even you, points out any imperfection in me. I feel so ashamed that I wasn't better, more, enough. Heal me, so that I can be at home inside my own heart with all its imperfections.

"Forgiveness is not about forgetting, Mack. It is about letting go of another person's throat."

If truth be told, I have spent most of my life with my hands around my own throat. To forgive myself, to release me from my own judgment, has been the hardest journey. Compassion breathes in the soil of self-awareness, the invitation to self-acceptance, and none of this happened until I began to see your smile.

"Forgiveness does not establish relationship. In Jesus, I have forgiven all humans for their sins against me, but only some choose relationship."

I know your forgiveness was "once for all," but thank you for not being content with that and continuing to relentlessly pursue us for relationship.

"Forgiveness does not create a relationship. Unless people speak the truth about what they have done and change their mind and behavior, a relationship of trust is not possible. When you forgive someone you certainly release them from judgment, but without true change, no real relationship can be established."

Now I understand why confession (to say to another how I have wronged them) and repentance (to change my thoughts and actions over time) are essential to relationship. Help me be courageous.

"When Jesus forgave those who nailed him to the cross they were no longer in his debt, nor mine. In my relationship with those men, I will never bring up what they did, or shame them, or embarrass them."

And yet I know you will let them confess to you what they have done and repent, like you have let me. It is a hard but wonderful gift that heals our hearts.

"*Forgiveness is first for you, the forgiver, to release you from something that will eat you alive; that will destroy your joy and your ability to love fully and openly.... When you choose to forgive another, you love them well.*"

I'll say it till I know it
Though it takes a million breaths
I'll whisper I forgive you
Till I loose this grip of death
That's made me once your master,
And made me twice your slave
And together we may some day gather
What's left of broken love
Climbed inside by The Tenderness
Of Lion and of Dove

From out of the darkness emerged Jesus, and pandemonium broke out. He was dressed in a simple brilliant white garment and wore on his head a simple gold crown, but he was every inch the king of the universe. He walked the path that opened before him into the center—the center of all Creation, the man who is God and the God who is man. Light and color danced and wove a tapestry of love for him to step on. . . . Everything that had a breath sang out a song of unending love and thankfulness. Tonight the universe was as it was intended.

"Forgiveness in no way requires that you trust the one you forgive. But should they finally confess and repent, you will discover a miracle in your own heart that allows you to reach out and begin to build between you a bridge of reconciliation. And sometimes—and this may seem incomprehensible to you right now—that road may even take you to the miracle of fully restored trust."

O h Merciful Wound-Healer and All-Forgiving One, please hear my anguished prayer on behalf of all the lost and broken. We are at war with ourselves and one another; we need a miracle.

*"Don't ever discount the wonder of your
tears. They can be healing waters and
a stream of joy. Sometimes they are the
best words the heart can speak. . . . This
world is full of tears, but if you remember I
promised that it would be Me who would
wipe them from your eyes."*

As you have healed my heart and shared your longings and affections with me, my eyes leak more often. Thank you for that. I remember when I could not cry.

"Is what I do back home important? Does it matter? I really don't do much . . ."

Sarayu interrupted him, "Mack, if anything matters then everything matters. Because you are important, everything you do is important."

Yesterday I slept in till ten, watched football, fed the dog, did some dishes, had a few conversations about whatever, and fell asleep in my chair at 9:30. Thank you! Every day is a holy day; everything matters.

29 DECEMBER

"Every time you forgive, the universe changes; every time you reach out and touch a heart or a life, the world changes; with every kindness and service, seen or unseen, my purposes are accomplished and nothing will ever be the same again."

May I see your presence as habitation, not visitation? You have not chosen to be Lord without us. Thank you for wanting me to participate.

If you ever get a chance to hang out with Mack, you will soon learn that he's hoping for a new revolution, one of love and kindness—a revolution that revolves around Jesus and what he did for us all and what he continues to do in anyone who has a hunger for reconciliation and a place to call home.

This revolution began at creation but is new to us; a revolution of love and a reformation of wonder.

31

This is not a revolution that will overthrow anything, or if it does, it will do so in ways we could never contrive in advance. Instead it will be the quiet daily powers of dying and serving and loving and laughing, of simple tenderness and unseen kindness, because if anything matters, then everything matters.

Father, Son, and Holy Spirit, I want to "be" inside your life and loving and learning from you as we live inside the quiet daily powers. Give us eyes to see you and your endless goodness as we bid farewell to one year and open our hearts to the next.

Contributors to These Reflections

Alexandra (Lexi) Young (OR)—a poet who sees beyond the surface, asks the right questions, and calls from others honesty and clarity. She is a translator: helping to bridge the gaps between people and their hearts.

Amy Young (OR)—a powerfully tender young woman, deeply passionate about all things true. She is a compassionate soul and able to enter into another's world and listen. Her perspectives are sure and solid and her call of justice deep and enduring.

C. Baxter Kruger (MS)—brilliant good ol' boy, Southern gentleman theologian who earned his Ph.D. in Aberdeen, Scotland. He's written a bunch of books, including _Revisiting the Shack_ (Winter 2012). You can find him at www.thegreatdance.org.

Danny Ellis (NC)—Irish singer-songwriter, responsible for creating one of my all-time favorite albums, _800 Voices_ (soon to be a book and stage production). He is David Wilcox's voice teacher . . . just saying. You can find much more of Danny at www.dannyellismusic.com.

David Garratt (NZ)—elder Kiwi statesman, who along with his wife, Dale, created _Scripture in Song_ and had a huge impact on praise and worship music in the '60s and '70s. David shares my heart for indigenous cultures and their unique contributions. More at www.davidanddalegarratt.com.

Deb Copeland and **_Don Lucci (husband) (WV)_**—servants with hearts wide open. More at www.livetogiveagodthing.org.

John MacMurray (OR)—a theologian and professional nature photographer whose work has adorned the pages of such prestigious magazines as _National Geographic_ and _Sierra Club_. You can find some of his work at www.creationcalendars.com.

Larry Gillis (HA)—a haole who has been my friend for well over thirty years and works as a counselor for broken people like me. On the side, he teaches people to fly. In my life he is a big kahuna.

Lisa Closner (OR)—wife of Scott, one of my best friends. Our kids went to school together, and we all still love one another. Lisa is a theatre major who teaches high school students the value of acting out, on stage. She and Scott are very involved in an orphanage in Honduras (www.wwh2h.org).

Mark P. Fisher (MD)—Mark leads a team who provide year-round retreat experiences on the headwaters of the Chesapeake Bay and, with his wife, Lori, is raising a family that ask good questions. www.sandycove.org

Pam Mark Hall (TN)—Grammy and Dove Award nominated singer-songwriter, she was part of the '60s music explosion. I met her in the late '70s, but she doesn't remember. Her music and more at www.pammarkhall.com.

Ron Graves (OR)—Irish Catholic man's man, who played semipro rugby for a quarter of a century, drives trucks full of toxic waste, writes poetry, and keeps the most beautiful journals I have ever seen full of art and words that keep me grinning.

And as always, a grateful nod to Canadian singer-songwriter *Bruce Cockburn*, the artist's artist whose lyrical genius is inevitably lurking somewhere in my words. He has his own Canadian postage stamp! www.brucecockburn.com.

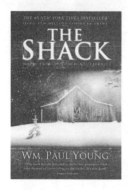

We invite you to continue your experience with *The Shack: Reflections for Every Day of the Year* by reading *The Shack*, the book that introduced the world to Mackenzie Allen Phillips, Papa, Sarayu, and Jesus, and *The Shack Revisited* by C. Baxter Kruger (foreword by

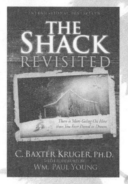

Wm. Paul Young), the book that guides readers into a deeper understanding of God the Father, God the Son, and God the Holy Spirit and helps readers have a more profound connection with the core message of *The Shack*—God is love.

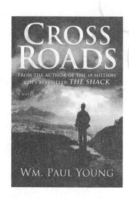

Paul Young, author of the international bestseller *The Shack*, tells the story of the miraculous transformation of a man caught in a purgatory of his own creation, somewhere between heaven and earth. A cerebral hemorrhage leaves egotistical multimillionaire Anthony Spencer in a coma. He "awakens" to find himself in a surreal world pulsating with a "living" landscape that mirrors the waste and loss of his earthly life. It is a horror he could never have imagined; an end with seemingly no hope. But to his amazement, he is given a second chance. He is sent on a journey back to earth, but one that will enable him to redeem himself only by using the literal "eyes" of several individuals through which he can experience their worldview, their hopes and concerns, and their trials. Each of these experiences will be different. Each in their own way has the potential of contributing to Tony's redemption. But there is a catch: Tony must use a special power he's been granted to physically heal one person. He can even heal himself. Will he have the courage to make the right choice, and thereby undo a major injustice he set in motion before falling into a coma?